DANICA'S REVENGE

DANICA'S REVENGE

Queens & Knights Book 2

M Kay Noir

Danica's Revenge (Third Edition)

Copyright @ M Kay Noir 2024

Danica's Revenge, First edition 2023

Cover Design @ Lerusha Reddy

For those who find beauty in the darkness, and for those who have not yet thought to look

...

(and for my loving husband, who finally found out what depraved things I write)

CONTENTS

Book Playlist   X

1. Carnage   1

2. Business   11

3. Kneel   21

4. Control   35

5. Brother   47

6. Schooled   55

7. Aftercare   69

8. Service   77

9. Seduction   85

10. Infiltrated   93

11. Outburst   103

12.	Double-Crossed	111
13.	Blindsided	121
14.	Liars	129
15.	Confessions	141
16.	Lost	149
17.	Prep	159
18.	Attack	167
19.	Protector	175
20.	Queen	183
21.	Aftermath	191
22.	Revival	201
23.	Forever	211
24.	Desires	221
25.	Gifts	229
26.	Insatiable	237
More by M Kay Noir		245
About the Author		247

A WORD OF CAUTION

This book is intended for a mature audience only. It contains often graphic scenes between consenting adults.

Refer to the www.mkaynoir.com/danica for the full TW/ CW list (on-page and off-page mentions).

If at any point this book makes you feel unsafe, please take a break and consider whether you want to continue.

Mental health matters.

B◯◯K
PLAYLIST

Listen on Spotify (also via on mkaynoir.com/danica)

1. *Hayloft II*, Mother Mother

2. *Lonely Boy*, The Black Keys

3. *Indestructible*, Welshy Arms

4. *Freedom at 21*, Jack White

5. *Honey (Are U Coming?)*, Maneskin

6. *Tear You Apart*, She Wants Revenge

7. *This Modern Love*, Bloc Party

8. *Dark Necessities*, Red Hot Chili Peppers

9. *Forfeit*, Chevelle

10. *Lydia*, Highly Suspect

11. *Figure it Out*, Royal Blood

12. *If I Were You,* Nothing But Thieves

13. *Frayed*, The Naked and Famous

14. *Outta My Mind*, Des Rocs & The Cobra

15. *Scared Together*, Silversun Pickups

16. *Nina Cried Power*, Hozier & Mavis Staples

17. *You Are*, Arid

18. *Doing it to Death*, The Kills

19. *This Mess We're In*, PJ Harvey & Thom Yorke

20. *Identikit*, Radiohead

21. *Smells Like Teen Spirit*, Malia J

CHAPTER ONE

CARNAGE

DANICA...

T he gates of the Fera mansion are flung wide open when we arrive.

They're never open—not like that. *Fuck.*

I wipe my hands on my pants for the third time since we got the call to hurry back, but they're still clammy. My right knee refuses to stop tapping, restless, like I never commanded it at all.

All the signs of chaos are unmistakable yet I still hold onto some hope that this isn't really happening.

Crunching tires on gravel is the only sound echoing in the silence, amplifying the anxiety knotting in my stomach. "Hurry up, Carlo," I urge the driver. But there is no point; Dante isn't home, not anymore.

The gate guards let us in with a solemn nod, exchanging looks with his colleagues I don't want to interpret. Their faces all say the same thing: we're too late. But I know that. It was already too late when they phoned us.

I wish my last words to Dante weren't "fuck you" as he kicked me out of his office against my will this morning, closing the door in my face.

Regrets won't help me now though, what am I going to *do*?

Focus, Danica.

The unbearable drive finally ends, and I leap out beforeCarlo can fully bring the van to a halt, almost tripping but managing to keep my balance.

"Miss Matthews, please be careful! I have to keep you safe!" the broad-chested Italian with the ill-suited buzz cut shouts after me for the umpteenth time today. They're always telling me how it's their job to protect me. *What about Dante?* Why didn't they protect *him*?

It's all too much. Dealing with a situations like this wasn't exactly covered in my public school education.

Tears threaten to overwhelm me, but I bite my lip to keep them at bay, pushing the emotions down. Crying won't fix this.

New faces are milling about outside the house as I run up to the entrance. They're shouting in urgent Italian and hushed English, but I don't catch any of it. It's been four months since I moved into the Fera mansion with Dante but there is only so much Italian my overthinking brain can process right now—and that amount is zero.

"Fuck," I mutter under my breath as I push past inside. My tough act instantly crumbles in the face of the scene before me. It's something straight out of one of those gangster movies my brothers would sneakily watch when my parents were out.

It's complete carnage in the usually pristine foyer. Two figures lie unmoving on the polished stone floor, separate pools of blood merging into one. I recognize them, unfortunately—it's Marco and Gio, two of Dante's guards. The unnatural angle of their necks and the way flies have already begun to gather tells me everything I need to know. *They're dead!*

"Miss Matthews." A familiar voice turns my attention to the right, forcing me to look away from the bodies I wish I never saw in the first place.

Relieved, I throw my arms around the old man, grateful to see him alive. Alive but not unscathed. "Emilio, thank God. What happened?" I ask Dante's second-in-command, taking stock of his injuries.

A guy whom Dante previously introduced as simply "The Doctor" is preparing to stitch up a gunshot wound in Emilio's leg. He's just like any other doctor except he specializes in discretion, Dante explained once when I watched the tall lanky old man with the receding hairline remove a bullet from Gio's arm. At the time, I remember thinking that this doctor had the longest fingers I had ever seen...

"We tried to stop them, Miss Matthews. But there were too many of them. I don't know how, but they knew about all the security, we—"Emilio flinches as The Doctor pours more disinfectant into the nasty-looking wound. My stomach turns, instantly queasy, and I have to look away for a moment as those long fingers do their thing.

"Where's Dante?" I ask, though I know there isn't much point.

Emilio shakes his head slowly. "I don't know."

"Who did this?"

"I don't know. They were Italian. But we don't know who...Or why." Emilio hangs his head. "We failed to protect the boss; I'm sorry."

It doesn't add up though. "He's usually pretty good at protecting himself. What the fuck happened?" I wonder out loud, wiping my hands on my pants.

"Something was wrong today. Don Fera didn't even put up a fight. He—" Emilio can't find any more words and I'm glad, because I can't hear any more of them. The dread pulses in my chest, tugging at the back of my neck like an unshakable bad feeling.

"Thank you, Emilio. I'm glad you're okay." He's not okay but I can't bring myself to say the word "alive." *I'm glad you're alive.*

Nobody stops me as I head to Dante's study, his sanctuary of power. It no longer looks sanctified—it's a complete mess. Broken glass, spilled coffee, bullet holes in the furniture...there is a puddle of blood on the carpet in front of the large wooden desk. I really hope it's not Dante's but I know it probably is.

It all looks *wrong.* There is no police tape marking the scene of the crime, no forensics dusting for prints. This is not how the Feras deal with their problems.

There are so many questions milling in my mind, but nothing makes any sense. I wish I knew what had been on Dante's mind this morning—what troubled him so much that he sent me away like that, without explanation? He must have known something was up.

I close the door behind me and lean against the heavy wood that, not too long ago, had provided no resistance to the unexpected intruders.

The anxiety pushes up into my mouth like bile, and the knot in my stomach tightens. There is no keeping it at bay anymore, and I breakdown, sobbing. *Oh god, Dante. Please be alive. Please.*

The tattooed god has become my entire world; I can't imagine my life without him. I don't want to. What am I even supposed to do now? This is Dante's territory, not mine. I am just a student.

Until a few months ago, I'd never even held a gun. Sure, Dante insisted I take lessons from one of the guards, and I've fired a few bullets. I am actually quite a good shot—a *natural*, according to Gio. But I am no match for whoever took my knight away.

My back still firmly against the door, I slide down until I'm sitting on the floor, the same floor I had Dante kneeling before, devouring my cunt like a good boy. But the room is empty now.

Despite the urgency of it all, I don't know what to do with myself, what to think. My 24 years of life had largely been spent in innocence, until the villain himself, the great Don Fera, unexpectedly showed up at my place of work that night, dashing as always in his expensive shoes and dramatic rings, clothes tailored perfectly to his muscular body.

But he's not here now to make a plan, to fight off the bad guys, to swoop in and save me. Who knows where he is, what they're doing to him. I have very few reference points for Dante's life that don't come from dated *noir* movies.

Sure, I play the strict Domme behind closed doors. I take and own every ounce of Dante's pleasure once he hangs up his boss-hat at the end of the day. But in matters of the business, I've steered clear. He's made sure of it. *I can't let you get hurt,* he always said. *I'm not losing you too.* And look now, *he* is the one who's been kidnapped.

Kidnapped. I've never known anyone who was kidnapped. The word feels foreign, jarring. I push it out of my mind; it's too unpleasant. Nothing good happens to people who've been kidnapped. *My poor boy.*

What I wouldn't give to feel Dante's strong arms wrapped around me right now, lifting me up to my tippy-toes and kissing me deeply. To breathe in that musky cologne of his as he begs me to please let him come...But this time, I'm not the one in charge.

As Dante forced me out of the house this morning (so rudely at that), I tried to console myself with the fact that my darling boy always came back to me again. When he was ready, he'd crawl back on his knees (literally), naked except for the beautiful collar that reminds us both he is mine.

What a magnificent sight—a 6'5" tamed King crawling towards you, emerald green eyes dripping with desire and locked on you (and only you) as a curl of his thick, slicked-back hair comes undone over his forehead.

Nobody else sees him like this. *What if I never see him like that again?*

No, shut up. Shut up! Why is the stupid game show host in my head always such a bitch?

There is a gentle knock on the door behind me, forcing me back to the present. It's Carlo's voice that calls from the other side. "Miss Matthews?" he asks cautiously.

I wipe the tears from my face, trying to keep my voice steady. "Just a second."

Before getting up, I take one more look at the mess in the study, the blood on the floor. Somehow, the little zen garden on Dante's desk had escaped the struggle unscathed, its peaceful pebble taunting me with its smooth surface, its tranquil vibes.

Don't worry baby, I'll find you, I vow as I open up the door. Nobody gets to lay a finger on Don Fera's body except me.

Nobody.

Two weeks earlier...

CHAPTER TWO

BUSINESS

Dante...

I t takes every ounce of self-control to stop myself from tearing the laptop in two with nothing but my bare hands. *Just breathe, Dante.*

For the fourth time, I look over the numbers on my screen, trying to add up the columns that don't add up. *This is not good, not good at all.*

"What's going on here, Luigi?" I speak slowly, my voice straining as I push back the anger sparking at the edges of my extremities, threatening to seep through my skin and engulf me.

The accountant blinks rapidly, the thick frames of his glasses failing to hide the nervousness in his beady eyes. He refuses to make eye contact, clumsily shifting his weight from one foot to another. "I'm not sure yet, *Signore*," he stammers, fidgeting with his hands over his round belly, probably praying to some deity that I don't blame him for this. He knows I have killed men over less.

"Our expenses are way higher than usual. Where did the money go, Luigi?" I ask sternly, closing the laptop loudly as I get up, towering over the little man.

Luigi instinctively steps back, trying to keep his distance. "We're looking into it, *Signore*," he answers, the intonation in his voice betraying his fear.

"This is not very good for cash flow, now is it Luigi?" I sigh loudly, trying to relieve some of the pressure building behind my eyes, but it has little effect.

The accountant shakes his head sideways, lowering his gaze.

"How did this happen?"

"From what I can tell, a large portion of it is the expenditure for the upcoming charity banquet, we—"

Raising my hand to demand silence, I cut him off. "That was budgeted for, no?"

Restlessly, I pace around the large room, running the variables through my mind. *Where did the money go?*

"*Sì, Signore*. It was. To the last cent." It's the truth, I approved the budget myself.

"So, where have the extra expenses come from?"

"We're still trying to figure that out," he repeats.

My morning is instantly ruined. Keeping the books on plan is crucial for the business's smooth operation. Not too much money to attract prying eyes but just enough to keep all the businesses going—those on the books and those off. But if there is not enough cash flow...that is a problem, a very annoying problem.

"I don't pay you to figure things out, Luigi. I pay you—very handsomely, I might add—to fix things. Are we not on the same page about your role here?" I raise my voice slightly, the tension weaving through each word, tighter and tighter, as I struggle to maintain my composure.

"We are, *Signore*. It's merely an oversight, I'm sure. We'll fix it. I just need more time. Please." I know what that whimpering *please* means. It translates to *please don't hurt me,* but the dweeb doesn't even have the balls to beg for his life properly. His weakness disgusts me, almost as much as his incompetence—I can't stand it.

Moving quickly, I grab the switchblade from under my desk. It's always taped there for easy access; I don't take chances. Before Luigi even knows what's happening, I seize the little bespectacled man by his collar, easily overpowering his short, pudgy frame made for the office and not the streets.

"Please," he repeats, barely audible, closing his eyes as he flinches.

"Look at me, Luigi," I demand, sliding the sharp blade over his arm and cutting through the fabric like it is made of nothing but delicate spiderwebs instead of cloth.

Luigi looks close to tears as he tries to meet my gaze. *Fucking coward.* I press harder, drawing a path of blood as the blade slides over his arm.

"I'm sorry. I, I..." he stutters.

"I don't like money issues, Luigi. Don't you know that?" I move the blade to his throat, resting it gently but firmly against his Adam's apple.

"I do, I know...Please..." The accountant holds his breath.

With a sigh, I lower my blade and push him away. He stumbles backward, into the coffee table, and trips, narrowly avoiding hitting his head as gravity does its thing. I don't offer to help him off the floor as he scurries to locate his glasses again.

The cut on his arm isn't deep, but it is bleeding profusely through the once-white shirt. It isn't the first shirt of his I've ruined. For his sake, I hope it is the last.

Counting to ten, I let the air filter through my pursed lips as I push back against the anger that threatens to blur my world into fury like it has so many times before.

For both our sakes, I turn my back on the whimpering accountant, staring out over the lawns as I let my mind wander. The silence is thick and uncomfortable, but I don't care, I need to think; I can't think when I'm worked up like this.

"One week, Luigi. You have seven days to find the answers. If you can't tell me where the money has gone by next week this time..." I don't need to finish my sentence. We both know that actions have consequences.

The relief on the old man's face is obvious. "*Sì, Signore. Grazie*. I won't disappoint you."

"No, you won't. Please leave before I change my mind. Send Emilio in on your way out."

He nods, rushing out in such haste that he almost trips—again.

Leaning back in my chair, I sigh. I've never enjoyed the business side of things; I've never enjoyed any of it really. But what choice did I have?

There's a firm knock on the door, three short taps—Emilio's unmistakable signature.

"Come in."

"Yes, boss?" Emilio asks, closing the door carefully behind him. He is an imposing figure, nearly as tall as me, but his voice is soft, deceptively calm—like Uncle Iroh from *The Last Airbender*, according to Danica (whatever that means). Despite his age, he is still a formidable force to be reckoned with. They don't make men like that anymore.

Emilio has been with the family since I was a kid and he was but a young man with a dark past nobody spoke of. When the others turned on me after I became the head of the family, I got rid of them all except Emilio (and the accountants). His role needed no name. Fuck having a traditional structure; a *consigliere* is no good if he's just going to stab you in the back.

"Have you heard anything from Luca? He was supposed to be here for the meeting with the accountant. It grinds me when he slacks on his responsibilities—" I stop myself from saying more, it's not appropriate.

"I haven't heard from him," Emilio answers simply. He knows me well enough not to add fuel to the fire. Although he's never said anything out loud, I know he's not the biggest fan of Luca himself. Some may find a lack of respect more permissible than others, but in our business, it is unforgivable.

"Such a spoiled brat; I'm getting tired of him not pulling his weight."

My affection for my brother runs deep, yet his knack for inciting a rage within me surpasses that of any other.

Emilio doesn't reply. We both know my brother isn't very reliable—never has been and probably never will be. I shouldn't be complaining though.

"Please send him in when you see him," I order, checking my phone for a reply to my earlier message. It is still unread.

The old man nods.

"And Emilio, nobody gets past that door, understood? I have some urgent things I need to take care of."

"*Sì, Don mio.* Understood."

I dismiss him with a wave of my hand and lean back in my chair, my mind overburdened as I twist the heavy rings on my fingers out of habit. A ring for each of my deceased loved ones, always there to remind me what I've lost. All I have left is Luca, the little shit that he is.

Supposedly, I can't entirely blame Luca for the way he is. What role model did he have?

Staring at the ceiling, I clench my fists, enjoying the satisfying sound of my knuckles cracking. I should work on not getting so aggravated; it's not good for my health—or so my doctor says (and Danica too).

I pick up the little rake on the side of the Zen garden Danica gave me to try and manage my anger issues. It seems so out of place on my desk, yet I've grown so attached to it. Much to my surprise, I like watching the neat paths form in the sand as the rake weaves from side to side in the wavy motions of my design.

It's not enough to calm me today though. Not even close. I smack a little black rock with the tiny rake, sending it flying to the floor like a golfer hitting his mark with a satisfying whack.

Fucking family

CHAPTER THREE

KNEEL

DANICA...

The nightmares jolt me awake more violently than I would've liked—again. They're becoming more frequent, as they always did this time of the year.

The cold sweat clings to my warm body, my breath still caught in a gasp that was supposed to be a scream in my dream. I know none of it is real, but the uneasy feeling remains even after the details start to fade.

All I remember of the dream is that I was nine years old again, running through a field that somehow blended the image of my childhood backyard with a nondescript forest. The twins (my brothers) were chasing me, threatening to lock me up in the shed again.

The rest of the story quickly evaporates from my mind. I'm not mad. The memories from those days are painful enough, I don't need dreams to remind me that my perfect childhood wasn't, in fact, all that perfect.

Picking up my glasses, my brain slowly processing the sunlight filtering through the slit in the heavy curtains that cascades down from the high ceilings. Dante always opens them a little when he gets up.

Maybe he hopes it will rouse me sooner, but he should know by now that I'm not a morning person. If I'm up before noon, it's a miracle. He, on the other hand, has lived a whole life before the sun even rises, starting with his 5 AM workout with Emilio. Rather him than me.

My day starts much slower, usually with a phone in the hand. But today, the notifications contain little of interest—the usual spam emails, a message from my mother asking when I'm bringing my *new boyfriend* home for dinner, and a bunch of other things I swipe off my screen without even looking.

My mother has been nagging me to meet *the new man* ever since I moved out of home. I'd only given her vague details about where I was relocating. The buff men (bodyguards) who had swiftly moved my belongings into unmarked black vans probably hadn't done much to put her at ease either.

But how do you tell your mother you're moving in with one of the city's most renowned criminals? It wouldn't take much digging for her to uncover who Dante really was; what he really did for a living...There would be a lot of explaining to do, especially around why he lied to her by pretending to be a cop that first time he rocked up at my house.

My mother has always been a bit overbearing. Maybe because I was the youngest—a full seven years younger than the twins. Always so overprotective...Yet she couldn't protect me when I needed her most.

Disinterested, I put the phone down again. I crawl back under the fluffy blankets, trying to find the motivation to start the day.

My bladder has no intention of letting me remain in bed though.

With a groan directed at the world at large, I fling the duvet off my naked body and swing my feet into the fluffy slippers waiting beside the bed.

I don't feel like getting dressed properly, I still need to wash my hair anyway (*girl math*). So, I throw on my short black satin gown instead. It does little to cover my hefty cleavage, but who am I hiding it from anyway? Everyone on the property is under strict instructions never to lay a finger on me. Not if they value their jobs (or lives).

The thought makes me smile. Dante's possessiveness is almost cute. Which is bizarre considering how off-putting it was in my ex. But Dante is different…His possessiveness doesn't make me feel trapped, it makes me feel powerful. He's not trying to cage me.

Shoulders slumped, I brush my teeth on the toilet, still slow with sleep. I am under no illusions that I'm nothing like the elegant women Dante is used to having around, the ones with proper breeding and pedigree, the ones who know how to get on a private jet and look unfazed—but I'm not bothered for a second. I know they can't give him what I give him.

Well, all the imagined women. Dante doesn't ever confirm nor deny their existence. Not that I mind. Everyone has a past. He's *old* already, after all. Though I would never call him that to his face.

The gown barely covers the top half of my thighs as I exit the master bedroom, confidently making my way to the study down the hall. I don't even bother with putting on underwear.

Nobody tries to stop me—they're used to me and my night-owlish ways by now.

Nobody except Emilio that is.

He may be used to my ways but he's still under Dante's command.

"You can't go in there, Miss Matthews," he says sternly, blocking the door. I always wonder if he doesn't get tired of standing outside Dante's study all day. Whenever I ask him, he just says that he can sit if he wants to, and that he does other stuff too. Who am I to question?

"Good day to you too, Emilio. Please move."

"I'm under orders to not let anyone in," he maintains, arms crossed over his chest like I'm supposed to be intimidated by him.

"I'm not just *anyone*, am I?" I try stubbornly to shift the brick house of a man more than double my size. An amused smirk tugs at his lips in the face of my growing frustration.

"Miss Matthews," he sighs my name in an exhale. "He's not in a good mood."

"All the more reason to let me in, Emilio." I know he has a soft spot for me. But it doesn't help me much now.

"Not today," Emilio almost pleads, carefully putting a hand on my shoulder to push me away.

"I wouldn't do that if I were you," I say boldly, looking him straight in the eye.

Realizing what he's done, Emilio drops his arm immediately, recoiling like he's touched a hot stove plate. Dante's touch-her-and-die speech must really have made an impression on all of his men.

Seeing my gap, I take my chance and dart under the guard's arm, slipping into the room before he can do anything to block me.

When I barge in, Dante is standing by the window, playing with his rings like he always does when deep in thought. At the sound of the door, he turns around quickly, an angry scowl flashing over his face. But it immediately softens when he sees me.

"I apologize, *Don mio*. I tried to stop her," Emilio says sheepishly, remaining by the door as I waltz over to Dante, victorious.

"It's okay, Emilio. I'm sure you did. You can go now." Dante smiles warmly.

I throw my arms around him as Emilio closes the door on his way out.

"Good morning, darling," I smile, reaching for a kiss on my tippy toes.

"Good *afternoon* to you too," Dante winks, kissing me deeply as he lifts me off my toes, sweeping me up in his strong embrace. As usual, he's dressed like he's about to shoot a fancy cologne commercial where all the men are decked out in dark lines and clean cuts. Today's look features another perfectly-fitted pair of charcoal trousers with a crisp white dress shirt ironed to maximum smoothness. His shoes (Italian leather) are polished to a flawless shine, matched perfectly to his belt.

"I was up all night studying." I pout dramatically but he misses it, staring out the window again.

"You can't use that one anymore." Dante seems distracted, distant.

He's right though—my exams are done already. But it sounds like a much better excuse for my sleepiness than admitting I once again got caught in the social media scrolling trap until the early morning hours while Dante snored softly against my chest.

I glance at his table, changing the subject. "Your Zen garden is a mess. Where's the rock?"

Dante points to a spot on the floor across the room where the little rock had been flung, a sad little dot in an ocean of carpet.

"Again? It's supposed to bring you calm." Shaking my head, I pick up the smooth rock and put it back in its sand pit.

Dante doesn't say anything, so guarded as always.

"Emilio says you're in a bad mood," I say casually as I hop onto his desk, completely disregarding the actual seating options.

"Is that so now?" Dante raises a brow. "I should give Emilio a talking to about what our trust agreement means..."

"Don't be mean to Emilio. You know I'm very *persuasive*."

"Oh yeah, especially when you wander around the house dressed like that." Dante shakes his head but smiles despite himself.

"You said I should make myself at home..." I grin. "So, are we going shopping today or what? I still don't have a dress for the banquet and it's less than a week away."

"I can't today. There's a lot on my mind." Dante sighs heavily, cracking his knuckles.

"That tense, huh?" I ask, trying to hide my disappointment.

"I'll make it up to you..."

I don't reply, letting the silence hang between us.

This is not good. Dante gets nothing done when he's this worked up—I know him well enough to know that. There is only one remedy...

"Lock the door," I finally say, my voice slow and sultry, commanding.

The entire vibe in the room changes.

Dante looks at me but doesn't dare to question me. He knows that look, that voice.

"Yes, Miss." He walks to the door and does as he's told. "Danica, I—" he starts but I cut him off.

"Quiet, *boy*! Stay right there," I instruct, slowly untying the belt of my robe. The look on his face makes me want to smile but I keep up the strict act.

Discipline is an important part of Dante's training. Our contract says as much. It says many other things too, listing all our boundaries, our maybes, our absolute desires. Within the confines of those papers lie the instructions for our entire dynamic...and those confines are not confining at all. He wants me to do whatever I want to him.

Still, I have limits I won't cross.

And Dante respects that.

Keeping his gaze, I drop the robe from my shoulders, the smooth material falling open around my breasts. Dante stands frozen, obediently, practically salivating at the sight. It's been a few days since I've allowed him to come. I know he's easily aroused now, just the way I like him. He is always more submissive when he hasn't had a release in a while.

I slowly uncross my legs, revealing the absence of underwear he should've expected but didn't.

A murmur escapes Dante's lips. I can tell he's burning with desire but does not dare to move without permission. Many painful punishments later, Dante is a better submissive for it. We are both figuring it out—me, how to be dominant; him, how to submit. But with each other, it doesn't feel like work, it feels like a natural journey.

"Come here," I whisper, summoning the tattooed god with my curling forefinger.

Dante starts toward me but I hold up my hand. *Stop.*

"Is this how you approach your Queen? No. On your knees!" I command and Dante instantly drops to the floor, eyes lowered.

Slowly, he crawls toward me, expensive pants on an expensive carpet—everything worthless to him except pleasing me. *What a beautiful sight.*

When he stops on the floor beneath me, I grab a fistful of his thick, curly, dark locks and pull his face up between my legs.

I always wake up horny and Dante never leaves that state. It's the perfect match.

Maybe it is because I can't ever get enough of him, of the pleasure he brings me.

"Look at me, darling." The command drips from my lips, sweet but assertive.

Dante's hungry eyes flicker with lust, with desperation, as he meets mine.

"What do you want? Tell me," I whisper, holding him there, face mere inches from my naked cunt. He dares not look anywhere but my eyes.

"To...to serve you. Please," Dante begs.

I throw my head back and laugh from my belly. How could I ever tire of seeing such a powerful man reduced to a whimpering boy?

The idea that Emilio is just outside the door makes it even hotter. Nobody has any idea that I'm not the one on my knees right now, that their fearless leader is indeed petrified, petrified of never being allowed to come again at the hands of his cruel Queen.

"I haven't showered yet," I say, releasing his hair.

Dante inhales deeply, almost panting at the revelation. I know it drives him mad. The smell, the taste...he loves it when I am dirty, he's told me before.

Dante whines in desperation, gaze focused on my bush. Who knew the great Don Fera was capable of such beautiful sounds?

Nonchalantly, I reach down, unbuttoning the top of his shirt to reveal his beautiful leather collar beneath. Nobody else knows it's there.

Hooking my finger through the metal loop, I yank his face into my pussy.

"Please me, *Tesoro*!" I lock my legs behind his back, pulling him further into me. A loud moan rises from my lips as Dante flicks his tongue over my clit, trained to perfection to make his Mistress come.

Without giving a single fuck that it's the middle of the day, in the middle of his work space, I pinch my nipples between my fingers, grinding my hips into Dante's face in a rhythm I know will send me over the edge in minutes.

Cutting through the moment, Dante's mobile phone starts ringing.

I smack it off the table but it continues to ring.

"Don't you dare stop until you lap up every damn drop, understood?" I hiss between my teeth, gasping between little moans.

The head between my thighs nods but does not slow down. I know Dante enjoys losing himself in my desires; it allows him to clear his mind. A win-win.

"Just like that...Such a good boy," I coo encouragingly in the teacher-voice I reserve only for him; the teacher-voice that instantly gets him hard, desperate.

Oh god! I can't help biting my lip as the pleasure builds between my thighs. My body is on fire!

Digging my heels into Dante's back, I howl loudly as the pinnacle of my climax reaches its crescendo.

But I don't let go.

Instead, I pant my instructions in hurried breaths...

"Every. Last. Drop. Boy!"

Chapter Four

CONTROL

Dante...

I t's difficult, but I try my best to walk like there isn't a vibrating butt plug stuffed up my ass.

Danica loves public play, but it always makes my life so difficult.

Oh god, why is it so uncomfortable?

How can I keep up the facade of being the brutal head of the Fera family when all I can think about is licking Danica's feet and begging her to let me come? What has she done to me? But I know it wasn't all on her; my submission has been a willing gift.

The mere thought of Danica roaming around with that powerful remote, ready to activate the plug at any time, makes me instantly hard. The anticipation drips from my sweaty palms. She will be here any second...

At first, I refused to let her come to the auction banquet, but her persistent nagging wore me down. She wanted to wear a fancy ball gown for the first time in her life and she finally had somewhere to wear it to, she said. How could I deny her that?

Besides, despite how dangerous the people in this room were, they operated according to a certain protocol, respect—nobody would be foolish enough to try anything at the auction; it wasn't worth disturbing the hard-won peace among the families.

The lavish foyer fills up quickly with the *crème de la crème* of the underworld, milling about in neatly pressed suits and uncomfortable high heels. It makes them look like ordinary rich people, instead of some of the most sinister figures in this city. In the lavish surroundings of the venue, they look right at home.

Dramatic chandeliers, elaborate artwork on the wall, the marble floor shining without flaw—a certain luxury is expected at these events. I don't care much for the dated decor myself, but I know the families are old school like that, modern architecture fails to impress them.

Not that I have anything to do with choosing the venue. Alicia organizes it all, much like she does my household, buzzing around with a clipboard to make sure things are running as they should. If her hair was pulled any tighter, her cheekbones would stab through her eye sockets.

I make my way over to the door to greet the new guests as they enter. More than a hundred people are expected tonight at this grand venue, excluding the security. No weapons at the auction though: there is a metal detector at the door that everyone is forced to pass through before entering the elegant hotel that was chosen to host the exclusive event this year (and only this year).

The annual Fera charity auction is renowned in all the wrong circles and a secret to the right ones. Large amounts of money exchange hands in the name of tax-deductible charity. Old debts are settled and new contraband acquired at an event that at surface-level appears no different from any other charity galas.

But everybody knows the millions of dollars that flow through the proceedings are not meant for the average-looking artifacts displayed on the stage under heavy protection. No, the real auction happens online through a very secure connection and exclusive access. It is set up long before the actual event, the bounties agreed upon before anyone even checks their weapons at the door.

$1,2 million for an abstract painting for Mister Marino, the paperwork reads. But online, the truth: "$1,2 million for semi-automatic weapons for the Marino

family." Power, weapons, drugs—everything is for sale at the annual Fera charity auction. The family's influence knows no bounds, and everyone makes sure to take advantage of their charity to stock up. It is the only way to keep the peace between the families, or some semblance of peace, at least. That and a truce around keeping the city's ports neutral.

The metal detector beeps by the door and I look up to see Emilio taking a knife off a guard escorting the Antonios. So much for the no-weapons memo. Every damn year, that metal detector goes off like a siren at a techno party.

"Don Antonio. *Buonasera*. Welcome." I nod respectfully, reaching out my hand to the bald man in the dark grey suit hobbling over with his two guards. His limp is getting worse with age, I note, forcing myself to not stare.

"*Buonasera*, Don Fera." The old man shakes my hand firmly, a forced smile forming around his wrinkly mouth. "Good turnout this year," he remarks, looking around the room. I'm not sure if it's a question or a statement.

My face doesn't show it, but I can't stop imagining the plug in my ass. I know I'm clenching but I'm so overly aware of it, I can't help it. Imagine what people would think if they knew. What would Don Antonio say if he knew the head of the Fera family was roaming around with a toy up his rear, completely at the mercy of a 24-year-old brat with a sadistic streak?

"Indeed. We have some desirable items on the auction list this year." Forcing myself to keep my expression firm but neutral, I hold onto his hand a bit longer.

Don Antonio just nods and heads straight to the bar, his guards right on his heels. He doesn't say anything but I know he's secretly judging me, judging the event—he always does. If there's one man who likes to remind me that I'm nothing like my father (as if that's an insult), then it's Don Antonio.

This is going to be a long night.

I snap my fingers at one of the waiters and they bring me a whiskey on the rocks. The familiar burn coats my throat and settles in my stomach, warming me from the inside. It's a welcomed distraction.

There is a sudden shift in energy, and I know she has arrived even before I see her.

The effect Danica has on a room is instant.

Though maybe I am the only one who is this overly aware of her presence...

My body aches for her every second she isn't near. It drives me wild!

It's only been a few months since our paths accidentally crossed, but she has me completely wrapped around her finger—and I don't want it any other way. Some days she is the only reason I don't burn the whole world to the ground.

Like the moon pulls the ocean, my gaze draws to the elegant frame of my Queen passing through the entrance, slowly, almost floating in the long black dress that reaches all the way to the floor. Fully mesmerized by the sight, I can't look away from the neckline that is way too low, her bountiful cleavage hugged tightly in the perfectly fitted dress with the corset-like bodice.

The gown is a symphony of black silk and satin, embracing her like a second skin. It cascades into a voluminous skirt that pools around her feet in dramatic folds, billowing with every movement. The fabric seems to shimmer with a subtle sheen, catching and reflecting the soft glow of the chandeliers above.

Matching diamond earrings and necklace round off the look, complete with dark eyeshadow and sultry dark-red lips that highlight her naturally stunning features. It is the most beautiful I have ever seen her look, and I can't stop staring, waiting for her to get closer.

"You can close your mouth now," she says as a warm hand slips into mine, trapping my gaze in hers. Danica is clearly proud of the effect she has on me, the bemused smirk playing on her cheeks tells me so.

"You look incredible," I whisper, wrapping her in my arms. She's taller than usual. Must be the heels hidden beneath the dress.

"You can kiss me. The lipstick is non-smear," she says with a smile, and I do so quickly, overly aware of the company in the room. I wish we were alone, that everyone was gone already; I want her all to myself.

"You look so beautiful in black." Enjoying the intoxicating scent of her perfume, I hold onto her hand a bit longer. She smells like lemons and lust. It's a new fragrance; she doesn't usually smell like lemons. But it's nice, I decide.

Danica squeezes my hand, and my cock jumps.

Hopefully, nobody is watching. So what if they were? It's not the first time I brought a date to the auction. It has been a while though, admittedly.

Danica shakes her head, smiling broadly. "You think I look beautiful when I'm literally wearing sweatpants and a t-shirt."

"That's true. You always look beautiful. But tonight you look breathtaking."

"Do you want me?" Danica asks as she does so often, her voice a whisper.

"More than I want anything in the world," I tell her truthfully, my other hand resting on the curve of her hips.

"Hmm, such a smart boy. Maybe I'll let you take this dress off me later." Danica winks seductively. Always one for games.

I lean down and whisper in her ear, "Thank you, Miss."

"How's your ass?" she whispers back, the words raising the hair on my skin, warm breath tickling my ears one syllable at a time.

"Nervous."

Around us, some of the most dangerous men and women in the city are enjoying their drinks and making small talk, completely unaware of anything amiss with their host. All they've seen is a beautiful woman entering and the intimate greeting I've given her.

I'm sure the older Italian women will be gossiping about Danica and I like it's going out of fashion. They've all been trying to set me up with nieces and friends-of-friends since my wife died. And now suddenly, a very young beautiful woman appears by my side out of nowhere...

She's young enough to be his daughter, they'll say. Probably not very smart with a rack like that...I don't care about any of that. With Danica by my side, I care about little besides keeping her safe—and pleased.

"Should we see what this button does?" Danica's lips curve into a suggestive smile as she fishes the small black remote from her cleavage.

Oh fuck. I shudder in anticipation, knowing full well what that button does. When she'd first bent me over her lap earlier this evening to insert the butt plug, I naively thought it would be a fun game to play. Bending over her lap is always so arousing to me. Especially when she is spanking me.

But tonight wasn't for spanking. No, tonight she'd carefully slipped a lubed finger up my ass—first one, then two—before guiding the new rubber toy into my tight hole. Instantly, my erection grew against her thighs.

When I'd gotten up, she made me stand against the wall, hard cock out and facing her. I was wearing my formal shirt already, my tie loosely draped around my neck, socks but nothing else on my bottom half. My ears burned in embarrassment, standing there like a little schoolboy before her, plug in my ass.

Danica had wrapped her delicate little hands around my cock and I groaned loudly as soon as she touched me. Nothing could compare to her touch, nothing. It's all I ever yearned for. Still holding on, she'd pressed the on button on the discreet remote. It looked small, harmless, but when I felt the jolt in my ass, I realized it was anything but harmless.

As soon as Danica had pressed that button, I literally jumped, exclaiming loudly as the first vibrations buzzed around the nerve endings in my prostate. The feeling was close to overwhelming. I gasped for air, panting, as I tried to keep my composure. But Danica just held onto my shaft, feeling it twitch and jump as the plug stimulated my hole.

Danica had stopped before I came, leaving me on the edge, pre-cum dripping from my rock-hard cock. She bent down, kissing my erection oh-so-lovingly—before giving it a hard smack that sent me doubling over in pain, crashing to the floor. No coming without permission, she repeated.

"Please, Danica. Have a heart," I whisper now, looking around the buzzing foyer. There is no way I can keep a straight face with that thing in my ass.

She pushes her body against mine, my renewed erection pressing into her. I know that's what she is checking for. She breaks into a grin, satisfied.

"I have a heart." Danica presses the button, putting it on the lowest setting. "But it's a black one."

It takes every ounce of self-control to keep myself together.

Every second is torture, and instant relief crashes over me when Danica finally presses the off-button.

"I should never have agreed to this." My voice is nearly a pant, strained from the effort.

Danica slides the remote back into her dress, between her breasts. "No, darling. You shouldn't have."

CHAPTER FIVE

BROTHER

DANICA...

"**A**ren't you a sight for sore eyes," an unfamiliar voice whispers behind me, too close. I spin around, ready to throw my drink in some asshole's face. But it's not just any asshole.

"Hello, Luca," I stiffly greet the Damon Salvatore lookalike in his well-fitted tuxedo and shiny shoes. He has that same lopsided smile...Not the eyes though, Luca's eyes are dark pools of obsidian that shift around the room restlessly.

"Danica, *cara mia*." Luca smiles the most charming smile I've ever seen. He takes my hand to kiss it, pressing his lips to my skin for way too long.

Without bothering to be stealthy about it, I look him up and down, studying his intense yet mischievous gaze, the way his short hair scruffs around his ears, the stubble on his cheeks. He is obviously a Fera, the resemblance is unmistakable.

I don't remember him being this attractive. We'd only met once—on his 40th birthday—that chaotic day it all began. That was the night that Dante's story became intertwined with mine. But the faces from that day are all a blur, all but Dante's.

"You look beautiful tonight." Luca bows gently, still holding onto my hand. His hands are soft, warm, almost elegant. I can't help but compare them to Dante's large, rough hands, instantly imagining them all over my body—first Dante's but then, involuntarily, Luca's too.

"Thank you. You clean up pretty well yourself," I reply. "Except for your face, of course." A fresh cut runs over Luca's cheek, down his neck, and into his shirt. It makes him look dangerous. I want to touch it, I'm not sure why. He looks so much like Dante but also so different. He doesn't have that haunted look in his eyes though, the pain Dante carries with him. It is a different pain perhaps.

"You know, this business we're in...it's a tough job." Luca shrugs, smiling broadly like he's laughing off a tear in his shirt rather than his face.

"I've noticed."

He squeezes my hand again, pulling me closer. "Where has my brother been hiding you?"

"Ah, so charming, aren't we?" I tease. "He hasn't been *hiding* me. I'm pretty good at hiding myself. I had exams...plus, you know, reading." I've never been particularly social, not for my age at least. If I could stay curled up in bed with my Kindle all day, I would. Some days I do. It's actually been so nice to have a bit of downtime after the craziness that was my final semester of studies.

I can't believe I actually did the damn thing; finished my degree. Well, I can, because I did. As much as I wanted to just play Dante's Mistress all day, I was determined to not make the same mistake again, to not give up my studies for some guy (even if Dante was way more than *some guy*). Not that Dante minded me keeping busy, he had loads of work to do too.

It was much easier to focus without having to worry about working as well—one of the many perks of Dante beating up my former boss and freeing me from that shitty employment.

Even with the extra time, it was a lot of work to get it all done, and the break has been quite welcome. As much as I wanted to go straight into my Master's degree now, I decided to take the gap year I'd been promising myself since high school. Before, I argued that I couldn't afford to take one. Now, *affording* anything was no longer a challenge. Not with Dante's pretty little black and gold credit cards in my wallet.

Besides, I didn't even know if I still wanted to be a journalist; maybe I never did. It was a good time to regroup and figure out what I want to do with my life, whether this is still me. The more I thought about it, the more I realized I wanted to have my own business some day. I was clearly not cut out to take orders from someone else.

But where does one even start with that?

The younger Fera pulls my attention back to him, almost with force, as his fingers play over my hand.

"I'm glad we finally get to meet properly." He still hasn't let go and I am lost in his gaze; I feel like the only person in the room.

"Luca." Dante's stern voice cuts through the moment. He puts his arm around me possessively. "You remember Danica?" He seems annoyed, his tone clipped.

"*Fratellone mio,*" Luca says affectionately, dropping my hand and reaching over to kiss his brother. "I was just telling dear Danica here how lovely she looks." He winks at Dante and I can audibly hear my darling boy clench his knuckles beside me. *Is he jealous?* The thought pleases me.

"Yes, yes she does," Dante says simply. He seems more stiff than usual, but that could also just be the toy up his ass. I smile.

For a moment, there is an awkward silence as the brothers stare each other down.

There is only a three-year age difference between them, but the gap looks wider. Mostly because Luca looks much younger than 40. It's that cheeky smile on his face, almost playful.

Perhaps Dante was a better brother to him than mine were to me. The bar is pretty low though. I was always the outsider; the twins always had each other. Inseparable since birth, born with an instant best friend. The golden boys, everything my dad wanted. A pair of athletic boys who excelled at everything they did—academics, sport, just life in general.

And then I came along, unplanned, inconvenient...female. My family had never had much money, but with a third child, we had even less. I don't know why everyone blamed *me* for it; I never asked to be born.

It was just unfortunate that the boys had hit their teenage years when I was still so young, so vulnerable. Against two of them, what defense did I have? *Wanna play hide-and-seek, Danica?*

Dante speaks first, and I force my wandering thoughts back to the Fera standoff.

"Where have you been?" he asks Luca, his arm still firmly around me, hand resting just above my ass. I feel like the perfect trophy and I can't imagine any arm I would rather be wrapped in. Though, for just an instant, my mind indulges in the fantasy of having both Fera men simultaneously. What it would feel like to have them on their knees before me.

But as Luca rambles off shifty excuses—clearly lies—I instantly realize that the idea of it is way hotter than the reality would be. Luca can never compare to Dante.

Dante replies to his brother in rapid Italian, clearly not wanting me to hear. I don't mind. It's boring when they talk about the business. Dante generally does everything he can to try and keep me out of it; I don't need the details.

Besides, a large part of me never actually wants to hear the details. I know Dante has done bad things and probably will do many more. Still, it is hard to reconcile the image of that man with the beautiful sub who climbs into bed next to me every night, burying his head in my chest as I hold him tight. To me, he is just a lost little boy—a giant-sized lost little boy...but still.

Luca tries to get another word in but Dante cuts him off, silencing him with an assertive wave of his hand. Always with the hand gestures. "We'll talk about this tomorrow. The auction is about to start."

Luca nods, accepting his brother's authority.

"Come, *Tesoro*, there is a seat for you in the front." Dante takes my hand and leads me away. Luca doesn't say a thing, his charm now muted. A frown plays over his face.

When I look back over my shoulder, I can't help but notice Luca is walking with a slight limp. I make a mental note to ask Dante about it later.

For now, I obediently take my assigned seat right in front of the podium where Dante is about to auction off the various items we all know are just for show.

With a mischievous grin meant only for the host at the podium, I slowly pull the plug's remote from my cleavage.

Time to have some fun, Don Fera...

CHAPTER SIX

SCH⊗LED

DANTE...

I t is way after midnight already when I slam the front door shut with more force than I'd planned. It shakes in its frame. *Stupid thing.*

"Jesus, Dante. What the hell?" Danica asks, trailing behind me, slowed down by the inconvenience of her heels.

Without looking back, I march up the stairs. I am relieved that the banquet is over, and I'm more than ready to get this butt plug out of my ass. Danica was selective with her remote usage, but still made my life very difficult all evening. It was the endless anticipation of her pressing that button that made me stress more than anything.

"Dante. Stop!" Danica demands as I reach our room. I freeze in my tracks. When she uses that tone, my body instantly remembers who it belongs to.

I don't turn around, just wait for her to catch up. A long, resigned breath expels itself from my lips in a sigh.

Danica shoves me into the room and closes the door, all in one move. "What's this about?" With a growing scowl on her face, she crosses her arms over her chest in a stance that I know spells nothing but trouble for me. Danica is pissed off. Once her arms are crossed...

"You've been moody the entire drive back." Her accusation is not unfounded.

"It's nothing," I grumble, taking off my cufflinks and setting them on the dresser.

"Is this about Luca?" Danica asks, perceptive as always.

"No..." I reply unconvincingly, turning away from her again. *It's not about him, it's not.* But it is. I saw how close Luca stood to her, how he touched her. Now that the event was over, the feelings I shoved down earlier were bubbling to the surface.

Danica laughs heartily, a sound so cruel to my ears right now. "You're being a child, Dante. A jealous one at that."

"I don't want him getting his hands on you. You're mine!" I finally turn to face her, fury flashing in my eyes. Luca is such a little prick. He's ruined enough. I'm not letting him near Danica. I've done everything in my power to keep them apart thus far, but tonight had been unavoidable.

"You're so cute when you're jealous," she says patronizingly, stripping out of the heavy dress that falls to the floor unceremoniously and leaving her only in a matching black lace undergarment set. Her large breasts spill over the top of the bra that could never fully contain them.

"I'm not jealous. I don't trust him." I feel like pouting, which is ridiculous—I don't pout. But a nerve has been struck.

"Fair. But you should trust *me*, no?" Danica asks, walking over to me. She looks stunning like that, especially with the heels.

"I trust you..." I lose my train of thought. Danica's swinging her hips as she moves, her eyes locked on mine as I gape at her approaching figure. I want her. No, I *need* her. *Dio mio!*

As soon as Danica is within reach, I shove her into the wall, my body grinding into hers as I kiss her—deeply, messily. I can't help myself. Her mouth feels so good on mine; she tastes of red wine and anger.

Danica puts her palm on my chest, trying to distance me. "Stay!"

"No. You've had this fucking plug in my ass all night, I can't take it anymore." I know I shouldn't disobey her; I'm being bad, but fuck that, she's been driving me mad with lust for too long.

"You'll be punished for this." It's a threat.

"It's worth it," I whisper into her hair between rapid breaths as my hardness grows between us. Her essence consumes me, I can't escape it.

"What exactly do you want, Dante dearest?" Danica fishes my cock out of my pants, stroking her fingers along the side as I forget how to breathe. Just like that, I know I've already lost.

"You," I reply, breath caught in a sentence I'll never speak, frozen, rock hard in her grip.

"Do we take things without permission in this house?" Danica asks in a tone a mother would ask a naughty six-year-old in need of a life lesson. It sobers me up instantly.

"No, Ma'am." I stand up straighter, trying to rectify my outburst with good behavior. But we both know Miss Matthews doesn't tolerate brats, my often-bruised ass knows it too.

She sighs and lets the tension hang between us for a second longer before making her demands.

"Strip, *boy*!" Danica tells me in an authoritative voice that would make me tear the moon from the sky for her if I could.

"Yes, Ma'am," I reply obediently, discarding my clothes in layers until I stand before her completely bare except for my collar, my hardening cock in my hand like an offering, a sacrifice.

"Whose is this?" Danica asks, slapping my erection with the back of her hand.

The instant flood of pain takes my breath away and I gasp for air. "Yours," I breathe when I can.

"Yours, *who*?" Danica demands, grabbing my cock and pulling me towards her, roughly.

Hypnotized by her, bewitched (desperate) I bend down slightly, my face inches from her—humbled. Usually reaching up to my shoulder, in heels she is less than a head shorter than me.

"Yours, *Mistress*," I correct myself quickly.

"There's my good boy. Now enough of this jealousy, okay?" She changes to her teacher-voice. It's sweet yet patronizing, soothing but suspicious, because we both know she has me completely hooked when she uses that voice.

I melt. She called me a *good boy*.

Dio mio, why do I want that so much? To hear her say that, to please her, there is nothing I want more than to make my Goddess proud.

Ready to give her anything she asks for, I nod. It has been so incredible to see her embrace her dominance like this. All it took was a few sessions with Adira to teach her what she didn't know, what she wanted to know...And look at her now, my beautiful Queen, fearlessly in control. Danica was a natural Domme. It didn't take much to refine her power—only a few weeks of private lessons that left us both sticky messes on the floor.

"Care to follow me to the play room, baby boy? It seems some corrective behavior is in order." She's still got my hard cock in her hand, toying with the tip, teasing it slowly. I'm so sensitive, her touch burns on my desperate skin.

Like I've forgotten all my words, I nod again, concentrating hard not to just come in her hand right there and then. As much as the impulse surges through me, I wouldn't dare. Danica would be furious, more furious than she already was.

Like an obedient puppy, I follow my Owner through the adjoining door as she leads me by my cock, pulling me along in a tight grip that makes my hardness throb painfully. I'm about to get what I deserve—the mere thought relaxes me. There is nothing I have to think about, to stress about, to feel guilty about...no, I can just listen to her commands and I will be absolved of all my sins.

Danica closes the playroom door behind us, locking it securely. Not that anyone else would ever come here. The cleaner is the only one allowed in, but only as and when instructed. Vowing them to secrecy, I had them sign a non-disclosure agreement upfront.

The large room is kitted out with every toy, every piece of equipment, every single thing my heart (and Danica's) could desire. The collection has grown significantly since the feisty hellcat that is my Queen moved in, but it had always been impressive—and expensive. Only the best for my Madame.

Danica knows exactly what she wants in the playroom tonight. She is always so decisive, so deliberate in her actions.

Meanwhile, I wait (impatiently) for my fate.

"You know why we are here? Do you accept your punishment for your disrespect?" Danica asks, and I know it's a statement more than a question.

"Yes, Mistress," I answer anyway, eager to repent.

"To the cross!" she orders, making her intentions clear.

I don't hesitate, I just spread my limbs against the padded surface of the seven-foot custom-built St Andrews Cross in the corner, my back to her. The hardness between my thighs press painfully against the cross.

"Such a beautiful ass," Danica says, slapping my naked ass cheeks—hard enough for the skin to burn—before securing me to the cross.

She starts by my feet and cuffs my limbs to the corners: ankle, ankle, wrist, wrist.

Having my back to her makes the anticipation even greater. I am powerless when I'm like this—almost powerless, except for the fact that she gives me *all* the power. No matter what happens, I know I'm safe, that I can stop it all with just a knock on the wood, our agreed non-verbal safe word. But I know that I don't want it to stop; I'm so incredibly aroused!

Danica's delicate hand slips around my waist, between my cock and the cross, and she takes my hardness in her grip, slowly massaging it.

"Was it hard not being allowed to come, baby?" she whispers, breathing into my neck. It's a trap, I know it's a trap, but I can't help but respond to her every move.

"Oh!" I exclaim in surprise as the butt plug starts humming in my ass. She must have had the remote in her cleavage all along—I forgot.

Danica laughs cruelly.

"We're going to make a mess of you today, baby. Just you wait. That pretty little head of yours will soon slow down to insular thoughts." There is nothing empty about her threat.

When she turns the remote off again, I gasp for breath—relieved—even though I know that this is only the beginning.

Danica's heels clink on the floor as she walks to the back of the room. She's selecting her implement, she must be. *Oh God.* I secretly hope it's not the rattan rod—that breaks my skin so quickly.

It isn't the rod. Instead, the leather strips of the flogger tickle over my back. *She's starting slow...*

"You know your safe words, right, darling?"

"Yes, Ma'am."

"Good. Now count with me. Ten strikes."

The flogger hits my ass loudly, stinging painfully. The first one is always the biggest shock, like my skin has forgotten what this feels like.

"Count!" Danica demands.

I grit my teeth, hissing the "one" through pursed lips. It never ceases to amaze me how such a petite woman can manage lashes with such force, such precision.

"Two" burns even more, falling on top of the first one and cascading into a burning sensation. "Three" numbs out everything while "four" completely empties my mind. By the time we get to "eight," there is nothing in my thoughts except the numbers and the blur of pain, the depth of the feeling as I fall through it.

A loud growl escapes my throat as Danica turns on the plug again, my circuits confused between the alternating pain and pleasure. She keeps it on for lashes nine and ten, leaving me so close to the edge that it takes every ounce of energy I have not to spill my load.

"Look at you. What a beautiful sight you are, spread before me like this, so vulnerable, *mine...*" Danica whispers the last word and I pant with lust. "Does someone want to come?" she coos patronizingly, gently running her fingers over my hardness.

I have no words to answer her, just moans. My desire to come for her is complete, whole. There is nothing else I want more, even though I probably don't deserve it.

"Not yet," Danica says, teasing my cock with her forefinger. I know there is pre-cum on her digits, I can taste it when she shoves them in my mouth moments later—I am literally dripping with desire for her.

For a minute or two, she just leaves me there, spread and desperate.

"Okay, little boy, it's time to purge all the bad things from your body, are you ready for me?" Danica whispers in my neck upon return.

The cold leather slides against my back as she reveals her next choice.

I hold my breath. *Fuck.* It's the dragon's tail whip.

"Is this what you want?" Danica asks, sliding the whip down my back and around, gently tapping the tip of my cock with the leather end. My knees buckle but my bound wrists keep me from falling.

"Yes…Miss," I gasp, struggling with the simple words.

"Such a polite boy, I like polite boys…I want you to come for me darling, come all over that cross. Are you ready?" She asks and I consent to the cruel torture I know is about to follow.

"I'm ready, Miss…Please," I beg.

I hardly feel the plug in my ass starting up again, because within seconds a painful thud lands on my rear with impeccable accuracy. It stings! It stings so damn much. The pain is blinding.

I'm in another world as the second blow rains down. My circuits completely flood as pain and pleasure mix in a single fury of feeling.

"I can't…" I try to tell her I'm about to come but I am incapable of even finishing my sentence.

Within seconds, my inevitable release explodes, thick pent-up cum spilling all over my stomach, over the cross. Every single nerve ending in my ass is on fire!

But Danica doesn't stop, no, the vibrating plug keeps vibrating as the next blow of the whip falls on my bum. I know she's broken skin.

Still, I hold onto my safe words. *I want more. Everything. I deserve to pay.*

The blinding pain blocks it all out. For a moment, complete serene bliss. I don't even feel the next blow, or any after that. Nor the plug's vibrations finally stopping.

"You're bleeding," Danica says after an indeterminable period of time. I can hear the concern in her voice.

"...fine," I breathe, the word heavy in my throat. I don't sound fine.

"Enough! Allegro," she calls my safe word herself, putting the whip down. It clatters on the floor, but it sounds far away. "You never use your safe words." I know she's shaking her head disapprovingly. She's not using her teacher-voice anymore, the scene is over.

I don't say anything, just collapse to the floor as she releases my wrists, my ankles.

"My silly boy...Look at what a mess you are." Danica's voice is calm, affectionate, warm.

I don't say anything; I'm not sure I can.

The world is quiet, finally.

Chapter Seven

AFTERCARE

Danica...

With great difficulty, I pull Dante's sleeping body closer to me, draping him over me like a heavy quilt made of muscle and tattoos. I love how his skin feels against mine—his fresh, naked skin. If the world would let me, I would stay like this forever, watching him sleep.

Mine. Finally mine. But more than that, I'm *his*. Dante doesn't just want me around, he *needs* me around. I finally have someone to worship me like the Queen I never knew I deserved to be.

To the rest of the world I am nobody, but to Dante—I am everything. And there is nothing I would rather be than Dante's everything. As much as he is my submissive, I am the one who feels completely owned. Owned by his desire for me, his need to make me happy. Is this what it feels like to finally be fulfilled?

Dante murmurs in his sleep, nestling his face deeper into my bosom. Such beautiful little sounds he makes sometimes.

Almost absentmindedly, I stroke his hair, placing a gentle kiss on his forehead. *Poor boy, so exhausted.* I can't blame him. His body took a lot of punishment tonight. I trust him to let me know when he's had enough, but sometimes I worry he doesn't even know his own limits. He's so conditioned to *just take it*, no matter what; endure.

At first, I used to feel bad for punishing Dante, for hurting him. I couldn't understand the appeal of wanting someone to consensually (and lovingly) beat the shit out of you. But now I know why he wants it, the need to atone for his sins, to free himself from the guilt, to take his punishment and be absolved—unlike so many other burdens he carries from his past, things he'll never forgive himself (and others) for.

Whenever I think about what Dante's life must have been like before, I just wish someone would've given him a hug at some point. Many hugs.

There is so much darkness in him now, so much hardened hurt, thick ugly scars over the pieces of himself he has lost, that were taken from him with force. The darkness cannot be soothed by hugs anymore. Not *just* hugs at least. No, the darkness needs to be dragged from Dante's body like a thread of pain that keeps unraveling the more you pull.

I feel hopeless in the face of Dante's hurt, the brokenness he guards like a family heirloom that is no longer precious to anyone, but has to be kept safe at all times. There is nothing I can do that will undo the pain he's lived. But I can give him the opportunity to control his pain now, even if it's a different pain, a physical pain...With a single word, he can make it stop.

If only he'd fucking use that word already when he needs it. It's up to him to define his own limits, I know, but I had to stop the scene; I couldn't bear doing real damage—even accidentally.

Earlier, after helping him down from the cross, we'd just laid on the floor for some time. Dante was breathing heavily, still lost in subspace somewhere. Giving him the space he needed, I just held his hand, waiting for him to float back to me in his own time.

When he'd finally found his way back to me, I helped his exhausted body off the floor and into a steaming shower. Dante had winced when the water touched his fresh cuts. Pain flashed over his face but only momentarily before he pushed it down again. *The things he must have endured in his life...*

My immediate instinct was always to try and soothe his pain. I hated seeing him hurt. But it wasn't the physical pain he needed saving from—the closer we grew, the more I realized that.

Studying him closely now, I regard the sleeping giant next to me with his arm wrapped over my waist, holding onto me tightly. He looks so peaceful like this, so content; the dark cloud that normally knits his brow and clenches his jaw is nowhere to be seen.

Even after all this time, I struggle to marry this peaceful image of a sleeping Dante with the way the world sees him—savage, bitter, vengeful. Yet here he is, the kindest person I have ever encountered in my life. I didn't think men could be kind, not until I met Dante Fera. Up until then, men had been nothing but cruel to me.

Sure, my dad hadn't really done anything—but that was the point. I might as well have not existed to him. His twin golden boys, on the other hand, could do no wrong. *What did you do to make them mad, Danica? You must have done something...*

Even when all the facts were on the table, my dad chose their side, everyone did. *Please Danica, it was an accident. Think of their futures. You're okay now, we got you in time.*

Their version of "in time" never matched mine. Their version meant I was still alive. *My* version of *in time* would have been *before* the panic, before the certainty that I was going to die at just nine years old.

We all still meet for family Christmas on the regular, that is the worst part. *Hush now, Danica. Let's just move on. Everything is okay now.* But it wasn't. It never was again.

I am safe now, I remind myself, trying to force the words to sink in, to feel real. Dante would never let anyone come near me again. The twins would be defenseless against his size, his ferocity. That's why I don't tell him what happened back then. That, and I don't want him to see me as weak (or broken).

I sigh heavily, pressing my forehead against Dante's. *My beautiful knight in unconventional armor.*

He murmurs in his sleep and pulls me even closer, hugging me tight like I'm his favorite stuffed toy. His semi-asleep cock rests against my thigh, and I reach down, stroking it like the beautiful pet it is. It instantly reacts to my touch, eager for more.

I smile, running my fingers lazily over his shaft before moving over to my own yearning desire. Slowly, I circle my clit with a single finger, cradling Dante close with my other arm.

Maneuvering myself (and him) a bit, I press the tip of his dick against my clit, rubbing myself on his sensitive head.

Oh god, the shivers! The wetness spreads between my thighs with every bit of friction. Since meeting Dante, my sex drive has been on max! I'm always in the mood now, ready to dish out pain and pleasure with a steady hand. Who knew people like me could also be Dommes?

I'm a far cry from those leather-clad, whip-yielding Mistresses I see on porn sites, but also, who cares? It's not like I'm about to start fitting into boxes now. That's never been me.

Dante groans softly, still lost in a deep sleep but starting to stir. It's a temptation too hard to resist...Even though I'm beyond exhausted myself. It's close to sunrise by now, but it's not like I have to go to work tomorrow.

Not bothering to try and be stealthy anymore, I move my body down, guiding myself onto his erection, finally pulling Dante out of dreamland.

It takes him a second to put all the pieces together, maybe less. The hunger in his eyes instantly flares up, and he tries to get up.

"No darling, don't move." I smile, placing a finger on his lips to halt him. "Go back to sleep. I just want you inside me." It's true, I don't even want to come, I just want to be filled.

Dante watches me intently as I lie down on top of him, his hard cock buried to the hilt inside me. My gaze is locked on his stormy eyes, freshly woken but fully alert. The way he looks at me—like I'm worth more than all the money in the world...I smile softly, pushing a strand of now-messy curls from his brow.

It's Dante who finally breaks our gaze, pulling my face towards his, muscular arms wrapped around my bare back. Neither of us move the rest of our bodies. We just slowly kiss, my lips passing over his eyelids, the corners of his cheeks, the tip of his nose...He takes his turn to kiss mine, the skin between my eye and my ear, my bottom lip, the wrinkle between my brows.

Finally, my lips find his, my tongue dancing around his in lazy circles like a slow waltz only we know the steps to. As I bite his bottom lip, I can feel his cock twitch inside me, but we remain completely still except for the exploration of little kisses.

Content, I place my head on Dante's broad chest, listening to his heartbeat as we drift to sleep together, his cock growing soft inside me again.

Home. I am home.

CHAPTER EIGHT

SERVICE

DANTE...

I wake up still inside her.

My body aches from our session last night, and the sharp pain in my ass is still there. But my body is used to pain, it doesn't bother me.

Instead, I focus on the feeling of Danica's naked body on top of mine. She is still fast asleep, face resting on my chest.

Careful not to wake her, I stroke her hair, inhaling her scent (a hint of lemon persists).

Wrapping both arms tightly around my sleeping beauty, I merge Danica's body deeper into mine.

I want to stay like this, my cock just resting inside her, perfect. But my own body betrays me. I have no control as my erection grows inside her. My desire for her is unquenchable.

Danica mumbles something incomprehensible, eyes still thick with sleep. Mornings were never her thing and this time we went to bed much later than usual.

"Go back to sleep, shh..." I kiss her forehead.

"You're moving," Danica says, slowly rousing from her sleep. She sounds grumpy.

"I'm sorry, my love. I can't help it." My cock twitches as if to betray me even further.

Danica grumbles some more, a drowsy child fighting to remain in their slumber. She grabs a fistful of my chest hair, almost absentmindedly, and tugs.

"Hey, hey, hey, you're starting early this morning." I smile, putting my hand over hers to untangle her fingers from my hair. Bringing her hand to my lips, I kiss each finger individually. So perfect, just like the rest of her.

"You're going to regret waking me this early," Danica groans, her eyes finally fluttering open. She stares up at me with that grouchy look that makes her seem like a spoiled brat sometimes. But the smile teasing at the corners of her mouth is unmistakable.

"Good morning to you too, *Tesoro*." I drop my hands to her ass, resting them on the curve of her behind. Normally

I would wait for permission, but *normally* I don't wake up inside her already, my cock warm and ready.

"You're waking a demon," Danica threatens but smiles nonetheless, reaching up for a kiss. "Good morning, baby."

I know she wants me too, the wetness between her thighs confirms her lust. She always wakes up so feral. Not that I mind. I could never get enough of her. Even when my body is drained of all its liquids, tired, achy, I still need more.

"We should sleep like this more often," I suggest, running my hands over her ass.

"It was a miracle that either of us got any sleep."

"I think we were sufficiently exhausted."

"Hmm..." Danica says, dragging her long red nails over my chest, scraping my right nipple. I flinch, inhaling sharply. My nipples are so sensitive, she knows. "How about now? Are you still exhausted?" Danica winks at me. *There she is. Good morning.*

"It's a secondary concern. I think you can feel how my body is feeling right now." With a wink, I pull her ass down lower onto my cock, fully. We both groan in unison.

"Ah-ha, I see..." Danica pushes herself up into a sitting position, hands on my chest. She gently rocks her hips back and forth, just once. "Is this what you want?" she asks seductively, closely studying my face as my eyes roll back in my head. *Dio mio, yes!*

"More than anything in the world right now," I whisper, arching my hips to feel more of her.

"Who said you could move?" Danica looks down at me with a stern face.

I love how her tits look from down here; they look even bigger. Instinctively, I reach out to them but stop myself before touching.

"I'm sorry, Miss. Please can I move?"

"No, lie still. You are my flesh dildo now; you don't get to move. This is about *my* pleasure, are we clear?"

I nod obediently, arms still outstretched to her as I make little grabby hands. Technically, I'm still moving but she allows it.

"Yes, you may touch them." Danica rolls her eyes, smiling at me like I'm a silly toddler with silly needs. It makes me want her even more. Especially because I know she'll never treat my needs like they're silly.

I eagerly take a breast in each hand. Despite the size of my hands, I cannot contain all of her, she spills over my fingers. Slowly, I caress her breasts, her nipples, exploring the soft flesh as Danica starts to move her hips again, grinding on top of my already-dripping cock.

"I want you to pinch my nipples, darling. You know how I like it. As hard as you can. Play with them," Danica talks me through her desires. I know exactly what to do. She's shown me before, guiding my hands with her own.

I study her face closely as Danica throws her head back, eyes closed, purring like a cat working hard at the biscuit factory. "Just like that. So good..." she encourages me, grinding faster on my cock.

With every movement, it becomes harder to keep my threatening orgasm at bay. But I have to. My Queen comes first.

One hand stabilizing herself on my chest, her other one slips to her clit. I know it won't be long now. Danica can make herself come in mere minutes—way faster than I ever could, no matter how much I studied her movements. She just knows her body so well.

Watching her face contort with pleasure, I am utterly captivated, unable to look away from that side smirk that always forms on her lips when she's close to the edge—how exquisite. My sole mission is to make her plunge from that cliff, shattering into orgasm.

But Danica moves her hand away, she doesn't let herself finish. Instead, she opens her eyes and shoots me a daring look. I know that face, she's just had an idea. *God help me.*

Danica puts both hands on my chest and leans down to kiss me, devouring me hungrily.

"Hold me," Danica breathes and I instantly wrap my arms around her. A knee on either side of my waist, straddling me, Danica keeps her hips rocking, bouncing on top of my cock as I hold our bodies close.

"Please, I'm close...Miss..." I can't take any more, I need to come.

"Not yet," she says, grinding me harder, faster. "Not yet."

"I can't hold it!" I can't. The concentration it takes to keep my body from exploding is immense.

"Almost. Almost...Just like that," she moans. When Danica pinches each of my nipples between her forefinger and thumb, I go insane!

"You have permission," Danica says finally, grinding into me as she pulls my nipples. She knows I love it.

Her words are hardly out before I release inside her, coming violently as every muscle in my body clenches and lets go. I breathe heavily as my cum fills her. Being allowed to finish inside her is a beautiful intimacy I cherish like the magnificent gift it is. Nothing beats that feeling; I never feel closer to her than in these moments.

Luckily, Danica no longer required me to use a condom, not after all our test screens came back clear.

Thanks to her birth control implant, we also didn't have to worry about making little Feras. It's not something either of us wants in our future, we've discussed it in great detail before.

Danica rides me for a moment longer until the overstimulation drives me to loud growls that rip through the room. This time she doesn't choose torture and only lets me suffer momentarily before resting her hips, just holding my post-orgasm cock inside her, sticky and warm—hers.

She gets up, standing over me on the bed, legs spread, as I watch my cum slowly trickle down her thigh. *What a glorious sight.*

"How about giving me some *service*?" Danica asks, winking down at me as she starts to slowly rub her clit again.

I'm riveted, unable to pry my eyes away from Danica's pussy as I watch her pleasure herself.

"There is nothing I want more," I reply. And there isn't.

"But first—you're going to clean up this mess," Danica grins as she lowers her cum-filled cunt over my face.

"Yes, Ma'am."

Chapter Nine

SEDUCTION

Danica...

Fingers gripping around the edges, I hold onto the headboard as I lower myself over Dante's face. With a thick thigh on either side of his head, I rock my hips to guide his tongue to the pinnacle of my lust.

At first, I used to worry about whether he could breathe when I was on top, but not anymore. I know he'll signal his safe word if he needs to.

My breasts bounce as I moan above him. What a shame he can't see it. No, his face is buried deep in my dripping pussy, lapping up every last bit of his own cum (and mine).

"Hmm, such a good boy," I encourage him. Like a sleeping predator slowly arising from its slumber, I can feel my pleasure starting to build.

I know he won't stop until I reach a climax, no matter how long it takes. Dante has been lost in my folds for hours before, happily so. But today I get there quickly. The various stimulations have been building since the night before, and in mere minutes I'm screaming his name and that of a deity that means little to me.

The bed rocks as I grip the headboard with all my might, riding his face while his lips bewitch my clit, building it to a point of sensitivity that's unbearable.

"Just like that, don't stop." He doesn't. Dante wants this as much as I do.

I can feel it in my stomach first—the climax that builds and builds until it explodes in tingles that run up my spine and over my whole body.

Without restraint, loudly, I moan as the orgasm reaches its crescendo. I don't care who hears me, why would I?

Dante slows down his movements, flicking his tongue over my pussy lips in broad strokes as he swallows every last drop of my orgasm.

"No more." I gasp, pulling his hair to detach him from my body.

With the last strength I have left, I bring my leg over and collapse next to Dante on the bed, panting heavily, eyes closed, as I ride wave after wave of pleasure spilling over my body.

I try to force my breath back to a steady rhythm but it continues to pant in wild patterns I cannot reign in.

Without having to open my eyes, I know Dante is just watching me, enjoying my orgasm too. But he doesn't touch me. He gives me the space to enjoy the moment. How well-trained he is. *Adira did well*.

At first, I dismissed the idea of getting a professional Domme to guide me as *preposterous*. I could figure it out myself. Why would I let some stranger show me how to please my man?

But Dante eventually convinced me to just come to the club with him once, *just to watch*. I hadn't even known places like that existed. My innocent suburban life had been nothing like the world of dark luxury Dante was accustomed to.

The "club" was more like a private mansion with different floors and rooms for any desire a deprived rich person could have. Dante navigated the halls like a regular; I could tell that wasn't his first time there. *An old friend*, he told the bouncer when asked who we're here to see.

My mouth refused to close as I gaped at Goddess Adira that first time—and many other times too. She is so stunningly beautiful. Not just her physical features (the olive skin, the long brown hair that curls around her shoulders, those breasts, the impossibly tall legs, her plump lips that cast spells without needing words...), it is the grace and elegance with which she conducts herself, the dominance that oozes out of her without a grain of forcefulness. Her movements are almost liquid, smooth.

That first night, I sat mesmerized on the couch with Dante's arm around me as we watched her command two subs. It was a private show. Nobody else had been there. The subs were male, both of them, and had their faces hidden behind masks. I'd felt bad for invading their privacy, but Dante had assured me that they got off on being watched and that we were actually doing them a favor.

One of the subs was a huge man, bulky, ripped—even bigger than Dante. But he crawled behind Goddess Adira like a whimpering dog as she led him around with a leash around his small cock. I had been spellbound, unable to avert my eyes from the scene unfolding behind the glass wall, watching as they obeyed her, desperate for her approval.

The next time we saw Adira, she was standing in our very own playroom, dressed in the highest heels I'd ever seen and very little else—just a harness that covered strategic bits (barely). Her body was perfect, toned, tall. I wanted to *be* her and *fuck* her at the same time. There was something so sensual about her, commanding a secret power that could be felt but not named.

Dante had been a willing guinea pig, letting us use his body as a test subject for my Domme education. Lucky boy. Enduring both pain and pleasure (and often both) as Goddess Adira had shown me how to take control.

She helped us set up the contract too, guiding us in naming our desires and spelling out the boundaries. There'd been a lot of *to be explored* answers on my list, whereas Dante had already been sure of what he liked and didn't. What he *didn't* like was very limited. His green list was far longer, including many things I couldn't see myself mastering—at least not yet.

Adira had come over twice a week for two months. I knew Dante must have paid her handsomely, but money had never been mentioned.

Such a Goddess indeed. There were times when all I wanted was for her to make me kneel before her, begging for permission to bury my face in her cunt. Many times...

I'm pulled back to Dante in the present as his ringing cell phone tears through the sensual memory. He sighs and picks up. It must be very important for him to answer now.

I watch his face change, the frown that gathers above his brow. With a single *sì* he puts the phone down again.

And just like that, everything is different—I can feel it in the air, the way Dante's breathing tenses in his chest.

"You have to go?" I already know the answer before he speaks.

"I'm sorry, *Tesoro*, I—" he tries to apologize but I cut him off.

"It's okay. I know it's already way beyond your usual wake-up time. Go." I smile, squeezing his hand.

In a single smooth sweep, he pulls me toward him again, kissing me hungrily. I can taste my orgasm on his lips and I lick him lustfully.

"Breakfast of champions." I wink.

"Such a crazy woman." Dante laughs as he shakes his head. "Where have you been all my life?"

"Probably under-aged." I grin.

"Good point. I'm sorry I have to go, darling. Trust me when I say there is nothing I want more than to stay here all day with you." Dante gets up and turns on the shower.

"I know, baby. It's okay. I need more sleep anyway."

It's true. By the time Dante is done showering and getting dressed, I'm fast asleep again. I don't even hear him leave, or feel the kisses I'm sure he plants on my face, my breasts too (knowing him).

After all our physical activities, I definitely need a shower for my tired, sweaty body, but I put that on my later-list, my body heavy with post-orgasm fatigue.

Sleep first.

Priorities.

I wonder what Dante's call was about but not for long. The Sandman isn't taking no for an answer, so I let myself drift into an uneasy slumber.

My last cognizant thought is a reminder to myself to feed Dante more cum, but the idea evaporates like mist as I sink into the fluffy duvet, letting it transport me to another world.

CHAPTER TEN

INFILTRATED

DANTE...

Twisting my rings, I pace between my desk and the window. *Fuck.* "Are you sure, Luigi?" I ask, not for the first time.

"*Certo, Signore...*I'm sorry. I don't want to be the bearer of bad news." Luigi keeps his distance, our previous encounter still fresh in his mind, I'm sure.

"How long has this been going on for?" I crack my knuckles, turning my back to the nervous accountant.

"A few months—four to be exact. Since we moved some of the banquet's expenses over to the dealership's account."

"The cash flow was better. It made sense to funnel some expenses through there," I remember.

"Yes, it was a good idea at the time."

Keeping the money moving was always such an intricate process. The complexity of it all used to break my mind; trying to understand all of the numbers and different businesses when I first took over.

I was so young though, so who could blame me? It wasn't about blame though. Nobody was happy to have me in charge, full stop. But they wouldn't dare challenge the will of my father, even after his death. Those who did were no longer in my employ (or on this earth).

Thank fuck for Luigi. As much as he annoys me, he's generally quite thorough. At least my father left me with an impeccable team of dirty accountants who specialized in money laundering (though none of us ever called it that). Luigi had been with me since the start. Just like Emilio. This was the first time any money had gone missing though...

"If it was such a good idea, how did we manage to lose all that money then?" It's hard to keep my temper at bay. No Zen Garden on earth could calm me down now. I am very tempted to draw my knife and finish what I started the last time Luigi brought me bad news. But I need him. Besides, I now know he's not the one to blame, merely an unfortunate messenger.

"Little bits at a time, *signore.* That's why we didn't catch it earlier. They used one of the company credit cards and kept the payments low enough to avoid being flagged. Five thousand dollars here, ten thousand there. Just slowly siphoning it out, paying fake invoices to fake companies, all with the same account number. It got lost in the day-to-day expenses. See here." He draws my attention back to the stack of printed-out statements lying on my table.

As I walk closer to look, Luigi jumps back, out of reach immediately again. So jittery. *As he should be.*

"And you're certain about *who* did it?" I don't want to deal with this. Not now. Everything is going so well.

"*Sì*. He had the card all along. He used it to pay for the banquet's flowers."

I lower my head and sigh heavily. *You can't trust anyone. Fuck.* "And the account? Where all the money was sent to. Who does it belong to?" I finally ask the question Luigi is clearly dreading to answer judging by the way he shifts between his feet, shuffling about like the carpet is made of hot coals.

"It took us a while to trace that one through the various shell companies..." Luigi goes quiet.

"*Who*?" I demand, slamming my fist onto the table.

"It's one of the Ricci family accounts, *Signore*." He's visibly scared of my reaction.

I stare at Luigi in disbelief. "It can't be. Why*?"*

None of this makes sense.

"I'm sorry, *Signore.* All I have are the numbers. The *why*, I cannot answer."

The sharp intake of breath burns my lungs as I refuse to exhale, trying to push away the darkness coloring my edges.

"Not a word to anyone, Luigi. Understood?"

"Of course. My silence is guaranteed, always."

"I'll deal with it."

Luigi nods.

"Go."

"*Grazie, signore.*" The nervous accountant scatters without any formalities, eager to escape unscathed this time.

Unsure of what to do next, I just stare at the stack of statements on the table, frozen. *Oh, fanculo!* There must be something I'm missing.

I start digging through it all again, line by line. But the evidence is there, black on white, undeniable.

A while later there's a knock on the door. I'm still deep in the paperwork, trying to find more answers than the numbers have to give.

"Not now!" I bark angrily, impatient.

This can't be right. But I know it is. More than $200,000 has been stolen over the past four months. It feels like I've been punched in the gut, betrayed in every sense of the word. It's the deception that bothers me, the lies. Fuck the money—there is plenty where that came from. But once trust is broken, repair is not an option.

The knock sounds again, more urgent.

"I said *not now*!"

The door opens anyway. It's Danica. But even *her* face can't cheer me up today. I'm lost in the numbers, my problem-solving mind desperately trying to make sense of it all.

"I brought you coffee, I—" she starts, smiling sweetly.

"I'm busy," I say simply, eager to get her out of my study. Having her around just makes me more stressed. She's a liability. I can't lose her. That's why I need to sort this mess out before it gets any worse—if it's not already too late.

"You're being rude." She looks at me accusatorially.

"Are you deaf, Danica? Not now," I hiss, hardly looking at her. I don't want to lose my focus; I can't afford to.

"What's wrong, baby? Are you okay?" She puts the coffee down on the desk.

"No," I say simply, stacking the papers on the table together. "You should go."

"Talk to me: what's happening?" Danica pleads but my mind is filled with a singular rage. Nothing exists outside of it. Not even Danica. I don't want her getting messed up in this. Transacting with the Ricci family could only mean bad news. They are the most brutal of all the families. Our on-off feud is a never-ending source of sleepless nights. I still have my suspicions that they were the ones behind my wife's death all those years ago.

"Go, Danica. I said I'm busy." I know she hates being dismissed but I can't tell her what's happening. Not yet anyway. She asks too many questions, questions I don't have answers to.

"What the fuck is wrong with you?" A dark cloud drops over her face. I can hear the angry tears threatening in her voice. But I don't look at her. We have bigger problems than Danica's emotions right now.

Without answering, I turn my back on her, walking over to the window, my gaze fixed on the grounds outside. *Maybe there's a rational answer for everything. Maybe—*

"Dante!" Danica demands, but I don't turn around. "Have you forgotten who owns you?" She can't maintain the authority in her voice, she's too upset. It wouldn't matter anyway. My mind is locked on trying to unravel a puzzle I don't have enough pieces for.

"Not now. Go shopping. Leave. *Please,* Danica. I need to take care of something. Maybe go buy yourself something nice, hey?"

I know I sound patronizing, but I'll make it up to her later. Once I know we're safe.

"Fuck you! You think I'm here for your *money*?" Danica spits, furious. I forgot how angry she can get, the fire that burns inside. Almost like the day we met. I smirk at the memory.

Danica is not amused though.

I sigh. I need to fix this but I can't do it with Danica here.

"Emilio!" I call and within seconds he's by my side.

"Yes, boss?"

"Please get Carlo to take Danica to the shops, I—" I start but Danica interrupts me.

"I'm right here. You can't just treat me like a child."

Ignoring her, I continue my instructions to Emilio. "Please take her to the shop but make sure she has protection."

"Yes, boss," Emilio nods.

"No!" Danica shouts.

"That is an order, Emilio," I say, well aware that Danica doesn't take orders from me.

"I won't go," Danica insists, crossing her arms over her chest.

"You have permission to drag her out if you have to," I add.

"You don't get to do that—"

"Now go," I repeat, waving them both away.

"Argh!" Danica wipes my coffee cup off the table with the back of her hand, shattering it on the floor dramatically. "You dickhead. You're just like my brothers. Fuck you!" She marches off in a huff.

"Please send someone to clean that up, Emilio. I'd like a fresh cup while they're at it."

He nods respectfully. "Yes, boss."

"And Emilio?"

"*Don mio?*"

"I want her out of this house within the hour. Understood?"

"Yes, boss. No problem."

"Good. I have enough problems. Go."

Emilio closes the door behind him.

I can't hold it any longer. The fury boils through my veins as I smash my fist into the heavy wooden door just to hit something. My knuckles crack but I feel no pain.

What a fucking mess.

Chapter Eleven

OUTBURST

Danica...

Despite trying to keep a strong face, I can't help myself—tears stream down my face as I run to our room, slamming the door with all the might I can muster.

I don't want to go anywhere, especially not the fucking shops. If only I could hide under the duvet and stay in bed all day. But within minutes there is a knock on my door, Emilio gently reminding me that we have to leave before the hour is up.

He returns every five minutes, threatening in his gentle manner to break down the locked door if I don't comply. I know he would do it too—Emilio takes his orders seriously. He can go from chill to psycho in seconds if Dante commands it.

Fine! I force myself to get up, to take a shower, to wash the smell of Dante off my skin. I don't want to think of him anymore. Yet everything in this house is his, including me.

As I gather my purse, I secretly hope that Dante is waiting by the door ready to apologize. But he isn't. His study door is firmly shut. *Not this time*, Emilio warns as I try to squeeze past him. I bang my fists on his chest until Carlo drags me into the car. *Assholes, all of you!*

Pissed, I slam the car door shut way louder than anyone can stand, but see if I give a fuck about Dante's cars. I don't remember the last time I was this furious.

"I'm sorry, Miss Matthews. We have our orders," Carlo says sheepishly as he turns around to look at me.

"You didn't have to carry me out of the house," I reply bitterly.

"You left us little choice," the other hunk of meat in the front seat says. He is one of the newer guards. I don't know his name yet and I am not going to ask it now.

Dante should know I hate being told what to do, and I especially hate being bullied by men more than twice my size. That feeling of complete helplessness is so triggering. It makes me feel like a little girl again.

"Just drive, Carlo. Get me out of here." As much as I would rather be alone, I know it's not an option. I am never alone, not after the incident at the sex shop when those attackers almost got me. To be fair, Dante was the only reason my life was in danger in the first place. I didn't need saving until I met him. *Well, that isn't entirely true...*

Carlo wordlessly starts the van, slowly backing out of the large, winding driveway with the rosebushes on the side, lining the paved road like we live in Downton Fucking Abbey or some shit.

As usual, we're stopped at the gate for a full vehicle search and retina scan before the heavy, nine-foot iron gate with the spikes on top begins to roll open.

"Where are the rest?" Carlo questions, pressing his forefinger to the fingerprint scanner.

The guard shrugs. "It's just me today. Two called in sick and the rest are out collecting debts." He walks over to check the boot.

"That seems irregular." Carlo is suspicious as always—it's his job after all. He surveys the perimeter through his dark sunglasses, almost habitually.

"It happens," the gate guard says. "The others should be back by this afternoon."

"Can we go already?" I demand from the backseat, feeling like a bratty teenager more than the Queen of this castle. I don't want to listen to any more business talk, I just want to be away from it all.

How fucking dare he throw me out like that? By now, I was used to Dante losing his cool but never with me, I'd always gotten through to him. Not today.

And to think how our morning had started, with him still inside me. Such a beautiful morning, so perfectly intimate, now all ruined. I feel so far away from him, that is the worst thing about this all. Like it was all just a dream now gone, I'm back to feeling lost, alone...*abandoned.*

What if he never comes back to me? Where would I go? Where would I live? Just the thought of moving back in with my parents again...I don't want to think about it.

Stuck with my increasingly negative spiral of thoughts, I don't speak another word the entire drive. Nor do I answer Carlo when he asks if I want some lunch. Not once do I bother even acknowledging what's-his-name, the new one, in his fancy pants and shiny shoes.

Everywhere we go, people stare, no doubt wondering who I am and why I am important enough to have two giant guards following my short figure through the busy mall. Not that anyone dares ask, not with the guards' gun holsters clearly visible.

I aimlessly wander around from shop to shop. Not too long ago, this would have been my dream—an almost limitless black credit card to buy me whatever my heart desires. Except it can't, because now all my heart desires is Dante.

Emptiness engulfs me, widening the hole inside into a dark abyss that swallows everything up.

So, I spend Dante's money frivolously, almost vindictively, as I buy things I don't need, forcing the guards to carry my designer bags through the shops. It's probably degrading for them, totally beneath them, but I don't care...they might as well be useful.

Despite not being hungry, I know I should eat, I realize when I start to feel faint. I haven't eaten anything since last night. The auction with its five-star buffet feels so long ago now. I stuffed my face with more shrimp than I could afford on a monthly paycheck and then some. But now my stomach is completely empty again with zero shrimp in the tank.

Without bothering to seek out anywhere special, I march the guards into the first coffee shop on our path, ordering them to a separate table so I can have some space.

I get a much-needed coffee and a croissant I can't get down, warming my hands on the cup as I stare out into the small space without focusing on anything. My thoughts are a million miles away when Carlo puts a hand on my shoulder.

"What?!" I snap, shaking him off. He knows I hate being touched without permission. What is it with men thinking they can just touch you?

Carlo is holding his phone, a solemn look on his face. "There has been an incident at home, Miss Matthews...I'm sorry. We need to go at once."

"What kind of *incident*?" I ask, peering at him over my coffee cup. The word *incident* has never spelled anything good. By the time something is called an incident, you know it's actually way worse. "Is Dante okay?"

Carlo lowers his eyes as he shakes his head from side to side—no. I know it must be serious if they're calling us back home.

"Is Dante okay?" I repeat, the cup shaking in my hand.

"We have to go, Miss Matthews," Carlo says sternly.

But it's what he doesn't say that makes the anxiety knot in my stomach.

Oh fuck. Dante!

CHAPTER TWELVE

DOUBLE-CROSSED

DANTE...

As soon as she storms out of my study, I know I've fucked up. I shouldn't have spoken to Danica like that.

But I can't tell her what's going on, not yet. Not until it's all resolved. She would just worry or worse—try to interfere. Keeping her out of harm's way is priority number one.

Still, the guilt sits in my stomach like a brick. Danica didn't deserve to be thrown out like that. I never want to hurt her, she's had enough of that in her life already.

Twisting my rings, I restlessly pace the room until Emilio's familiar knock drags me out of the mental spiral of guilt with a fresh cup of coffee that he places on my desk with a simple nod.

"Taking on new tasks?" I try to smile but the attempt is largely unsuccessful.

"I didn't make it, I'm just bringing it in." The big man's voice shows no humor, it rarely does.

I raise an eyebrow. "Oh?"

"They're too scared, boss."

"And why is that?" I know the answer but I want him to tell me.

"Miss Matthews was quite upset earlier..." he carefully broaches the subject.

Emilio is more than just my guard. He is my confidant, my advisor. In the more than two decades we've worked together, Emilio has been the most dependable person in my life.

"Yes, I suppose so. I have a lot on my mind..."

"You don't have to explain yourself to me, *Don mio*," Emilio says simply, formal as always.

"I should make it up to her though. Will you speak to Alicia please and arrange a special dinner for tonight? Just here at home. It's not safe to go out."

If anyone can pull something together last-minute, Alicia can. My house manager slash personal assistant has only been with the family for three years now, but she's proved a quick learner. Dependable and efficient is a winning combination in such a role.

"Yes, *boss.*"

"And ask her to get some of Danica's favorite flowers too, those dark red tulips. Make it special, you know?" I am trying, but romantic isn't really my style. Not since my wife died...More than six years ago now. I flinch at the mere thought of those days.

Emilio nods.

"And please keep that door closed at all times."

"Of course." Emilio quietly takes his leave without question, resuming his post right outside. I wish I could clone that man; having multiple Emilios would make my life much easier.

Maybe if Emilio had been at home that day, rather than with me, my wife would still be alive. I can't stop the thoughts that drift to the painful past, poking a raw wound that never seems to close. Poking it just to make sure it still hurts. It does. A lot.

Elena.

Sometimes, on warm Spring afternoons, I can still hear her laugh echoing through the rooms of the mansion. She made it all feel so different, the whole house, my life. Things had been dark until she'd come along with those long legs and innocent smile, dark curls cascading down her back.

Elena was made of pure sunshine, beautiful in every sense of the word. A true Italian too, my dad would have been proud. No, my dad was never proud. But he *could* have been.

When I told Danica the story, she just threw her arms around me, crying as she held me. I wanted to cry too, but I couldn't. It was the first time I had spoken about Elena since the day I lost her, more than six years ago now.

I had just turned 32 when we met (Elena was 26). She was Don Greco's youngest daughter, a suitable match. From the moment I'd first laid eyes on her at some social gathering I didn't care for, I couldn't tear myself away from her.

Our attraction had been instant. She wanted me as much as I wanted her. Elena had been used to the crime life; I didn't have to hide anything from her. She loved me as I was. For the first time since taking over the family business 13 years prior, I had found something that was purely mine.

Elena had been the most beautifully obedient sub any man could wish for. The way she kneeled for me, waiting by the door every day, naked except for her collar. The things she let me do to her body, the things she wanted me to do...

Her devotion had known no bounds. And neither had my desire for her. I wanted her all the time, wanted to make her face contort in pleasure as she screamed my name loud enough for everyone in the house to hear.

I had never been a pleasure Dom until I met Elena. But her satisfaction became the only thing that mattered to me. We married within two years in an extravagant affair attended by both families en masse. I will never forget the sight of her walking up in that pure white dress, the smile she wore just for me. We were so happy. So naive too, in hindsight.

I was going to give it all up for her; I was going to get out...maybe move back to Italy, start a family of our own. Luca could take over. He was keen for the power but not so keen to learn. Still, I'd been ready to hand it all over to him, even if he burned it all to the ground. Anything to take my princess away to another castle, to keep her safe.

I'd wanted nothing more than to live by the sea in a modest house, just us, maybe a few kids running around. For a moment, I'd thought I could have it all, that I could be just Dante, not Don Fera.

But nobody gets out alive.

Emilio had been with me the day it happened. We'd gone to bail out Luca again after some or other dumb shit he'd gotten himself into. I don't know if I've ever stopped resenting him, or myself, for not having been there when they took her that day.

Elena had gone to the doctor. A guard was with her, as always. Only much later did I find out she was pregnant. We were meant to have a little boy. I couldn't bring myself to tell Danica this part, not yet.

The guard hadn't been able to defend Elena by himself, outnumbered. They'd taken her.

I still don't know who did it or why. Nobody has ever owned up to the act. I suspect it was the Riccis, but I can't prove it.

It had taken too long to find her. By the time I did, I could no longer save her. They'd left her butchered on the cold floor, naked, bleeding out over the concrete in some abandoned building, her beautiful face desecrated by ugly cuts and bruises.

That had been the first time I cried since my mother died. Elena's body was cold, lifeless, as I picked her up, blood smeared across my shirt, my hands. I cried into her messy hair. Cried for the life we could've had, the life that was lost. Only Emilio had seen me fall apart. But we never spoken about it again.

With a heavy sigh, I kissed the ruby on the ring adorning my right hand. Sweet dear Elena.

Focus, Dante! The painful ghosts of my past won't solve my current predicament. I need to find a way to handle this swiftly and discreetly.

With three big gulps, I finish my lukewarm coffee and check my phone again. Still nothing.

I try to call him again but it just rings. My text remains unread as well.

You fucker. What have you gotten yourself mixed up in now?

I'm still contemplating my next move when I hear a gunshot outside. It's muffled but unmistakable, a dull thud that reverberates through the thick walls of my office. The sudden sound sends a jolt of adrenaline through my veins.

What the fuck?

Instinctively, I open the desk drawer and fish out my gun, the cold metal reassuringly familiar in my hand. My fingers tremble as I try to check that it's loaded, but my vision suddenly blurs. My head feels like it's filled with cotton; I can't focus on the simple task I've performed thousands of times before.

Get it together, Dante! I command myself, taking a deep breath in a desperate attempt to clear the fog clouding my thoughts.

Outside, chaos erupts. Shouts in rapid, frantic Italian pierce the air, and I catch fragments of Emilio's voice, but I can't make out the words.

More gunshots ring out, louder this time, echoing like thunderclaps through the corridor.

I don't know what's going on. *Where are the guards? Emilio?*

Moments later, my door bursts open with the deafening crash of splintering wood. An army of masked gunmen floods into my office, their black-clad forms moving with military precision.

Panic claws at my chest as I scramble to raise my gun, but I'm too slow.

I fire a shot but not before they do. Blinding pain burns through me, and I drop the gun, clutching at my shoulder as hot blood seeps between my fingers. I try to focus, to count the armed men swarming into my study, but my mind is sluggish, unable to keep up with the rapid onslaught.

There are eight of them, maybe more. Their shouts are unmistakably Italian, but the voices are unfamiliar.

They grab me from behind the desk. I try to struggle but it's no use, my limbs feel like lead—heavy and unresponsive. Desperation surges through me, a primal instinct to survive, but it's no use. A blow lands on my jaw, the sharp impact of a pistol butt sending me crashing to the floor.

The world tilts and spins, and I taste blood, metallic and bitter, in my mouth.

I lie there, dazed and helpless, as the one asshole points his gun to my forehead.

No!

CHAPTER THIRTEEN

BLINDSIDED

DANTE...

When I finally come to, I have no idea where I am. My mind races, tangled thoughts grappling for clarity, but one thing cuts through the fog with fierce urgency: I have to find Danica.

Try as I might, I can't see a thing; the blackest of dark surrounds me in all directions. I don't remember being blindfolded, but then again, I don't remember a lot of things.

My head is fuzzy, dazed, like I'd been chasing white lines from dusk to dawn, the sunrises dripping in reckless abandon like they used to do during my youthful Vegas party days. But my nose has been a one-way street for years now, so I know it's not recreational drugs.

Pain pulses through my bruised body as I'm jolted back to consciousness. My face is sticky, warm; the familiar feeling of drying blood clings to my skin, its coppery taste on my tongue. The worst is my shoulder, it's on fire!

I try to wipe my cheek but my arm won't obey any commands. Only when I try again without any result do I realize I can't move at all.

Ropes, it's ropes. Rough ropes are cutting into my wrists. Whoever tied me up did a good job, there isn't even the smallest wiggle room—I am secured fully to what feels like the world's most uncomfortable chair.

My body is too big for chairs like this, those stupid fold-up metal ones that were more for function than comfort. I doubt my comfort was of anyone's concern currently though.

The oppressive darkness presses in, amplifying the silence around me. I strain to hear anything, any sign of where I might be or who might be near, but the void offers no answers. Fear gnaws at me, each minute passing by in a torturous eternity. *It's hopeless.*

But I can't give up. I have to get to Danica before they do. It might already be too late...This is not how this story is supposed to go. Not now. Not when things are finally starting to come together again. I grit my teeth, forcing the pain and fear to the back of my mind. There has to be a way out. There has to be a way to save her.

"Untie me, assholes!" I demand, my voice failing to convey the authority I intended. It sounds weak, hoarse...foreign. *I need water.*

There is no response from the empty room that reeks of sourness, like someone puked on the floor weeks ago and simply left it to dry. The scent is intoxicating and not in a sexy way—quite the opposite.

"You're going to regret this," I try again but my threat falls on deaf ears. My voice echoes back to me in the cold room with the floor that feels like rough concrete beneath my bare feet. Definitely not a luxury accommodation, though I doubt I am here on a social call. You don't just kidnap a Don for *fun*...

Desperate for freedom, I rock back and forth, trying to tip the metal chair, but it's no use—it appears to be bolted to the floor. *Fuckers.* I wish I knew who they were but the assholes are too cowardly to even show their faces, to answer my threats.

I struggle for a few minutes more before my broken body forces me to accept the limitations of my situation. Even the slightest move tugs at my burning shoulder like a knife stabbing through my skin again and again.

How did this even happen? I still can't piece it all together.

I remember sending Danica away. I remember joking with Emilio about the coffee. And then, suddenly, a huge commotion outside my study. Gunshots. So many gunshots—they still ring in my sore ears.

I know I'd jumped up, drawing my weapon, ready to destroy whoever dared invade my home. But my movements had been slow, fuzzy. Too slow. I never stood a chance.

I'd fumbled too long and the invaders got me in the shoulder, a clean shot that went right through me—a small mercy at least. They pinned me to the floor and kicked the shit out of me before I could take out a single one of them.

That much came back to me. But I don't know how much time has passed since I blacked out in a pool of my own blood. Was it this morning? It could have been yesterday too, but I really hope it wasn't.

The last thing I remember was one of the armed men in my study grabbing my hair, pulling my bloodied face off the floor. His Italian had been flawless. Native. *Curse you and your whole family, Don Fera,* he said, spitting in my eye before smashing my face into the floor...

There is nothing in my memory after that, nothing but all-encompassing darkness.

What happened though? The attackers should never have even gotten as far as my study. That has never happened before—not in all the decades the Fera family have lived on that property. We have layers of security, guards patrolling the grounds, and secret access codes that change regularly.

How did they get in? The answer is obvious but it's not one I want to accept. There is no way into the fortress that is the Fera house without insider access. Even then, it would be near impossible to get past the various guards.

Someone in my inner circle has betrayed me. I sincerely hope my suspicions are wrong, and that everything isn't connected. Because if I'm right, Danica is in even more danger than I thought.

The thought of Danica in trouble sends a fresh wave of urgency coursing through me. My heart pounds in my chest, a rhythmic reminder that time is slipping away. I can't shake the image of her in peril, her life hanging in the balance because of a betrayal I never saw coming.

I need to get to her...My beautiful *Tesoro*. I wish my last words to her hadn't been so cruel. She didn't deserve it. She doesn't deserve any of this.

What I wouldn't give to be home in her arms, wrapped around her petite frame, face buried in those large breasts I loved to suck on. She would take her black-rimmed reading glasses off, the ones that made her look like a high school teacher, push her hair behind her ears, and kiss my forehead as she'd done a million times before. She would tell me it's all okay, that we're safe.

But we aren't safe.

We aren't safe *at all*.

Groaning loudly, I pull on the ropes with all my might, desperate for freedom. But it's no use. The only result is the blinding pain in my shoulder damn near knocking me out again.

Oh, fanculo.

CHAPTER FOURTEEN

LIARS

DANICA...

It's been two nights since they took Dante. Two tormented sleepless nights without my *Tesoro*, my treasure.

Trying to keep it steady, I hold my steaming coffee cup with both hands but can't bring myself to drink it. I came to hide out in the library, my usual place of refuge, hoping to find some escape, some peace but all I found was a Dante-sized hole.

Focus blurred, I stare out over the lawns as my feelings toggle between desperate, lost, exhausted, and a million other emotions I don't have the name (or energy for.) Above all, I am sick with worry—it lies heavy in my stomach like a breath I cannot catch; I'm drowning.

This is the longest Dante and I have ever been apart since we met. I don't know what to do with myself, I feel so useless. Emilio and Luca have been out all day, speaking to some of the family's informants, hoping to find something, anything, about who took Dante or why. They didn't want me to come with though—*You'll just be in the way, Danica*. As always.

With Dante away, everyone accepts Emilio's authority—despite Luca's weak demands to be treated like the boss. I'm glad to have the older man in charge. If only there was something I could do to be useful, but I'm frozen, on pause.

I try to keep my mind from the worst-case scenario but it's difficult. Dante has a lot of enemies, enemies capable of things I cannot even fathom. He has shielded me from the horrors of the business as much as he could, but who was there to protect him?

I can't stay in our room. It feels so empty. *What if he never comes back?* If only I could stop asking myself that.

Another thing has been taken from me. *You can't have nice things, Danica, don't you learn?* My inner voice has never been kind. As ugly inside as I am out—or at least that's how I used to see myself. That's what everyone made me believe. My father, my brothers, that fuck-head ex who I gave up my studies for.

But not Dante. In his eyes, I am always beautiful, perfect. He believes it so much that I almost started believing it too. I want to be who he sees me as; I am better with him...no, *for* him. A god like Dante Fera deserves a Queen worthy of worship.

But I am a useless Monarch. I can't do anything to bring my Knight back. I want to cry but I have no more tears left; I'm all cried out.

"You ever going to drink that coffee?" A familiar voice pulls me back to the high-ceilinged room stacked top-to-bottom with beautiful books I should read to distract myself but they hold no appeal when my tumultuous mind seeks only one solace—Dante.

"Any news?" I ask hopefully, turning to Luca.

"Nothing. We've spoken to all the families but nobody knows shit." He puts a hand on my shoulder but I feel no comfort.

I imagine I must look like a complete mess, I feel like one. It's been days since I last showered, not since Dante left, and my hair is tied up in a messy ponytail, my thick glasses pushed over my face. Why bother with the contact lenses now? *Why bother with anything?*

Luca puts an arm around me and pulls me out of the chair, pressing me against his body. His breath reeks of alcohol, a foul smell that hangs heavy in the air, assaulting my senses.

"It will be okay—" Luca starts, letting his hand drop to my ass.

As if stung by a bee, I instantly recoil from him.

"Jesus, Luca!" I exclaim, pushing him back in disgust.

There is nothing consensual about Luca's advances and I'm not here for it, not at all. His touch makes me want to pour boiling water on my skin just to get rid of his slimy fingerprints. How could I have ever imagined him desirable, even for a second, at the auction?

Whatever attractive physical attributes the younger Fera had been blessed with were overshadowed by his shifty personality that became more repulsive the longer you spent in his presence.

Fuck Luca; he could never stand in for Dante. What I wouldn't give to have my darling boy hold me tight again, to hear the word *Tesoro* drip from his lips in that deep voice of his...I just need Dante to come back and then everything will be okay. But he's not here to save me any more than I can save him right now.

Luca grabs my wrist, and I glare daggers into his eyes, desperately trying to shake him loose. "Let go," I hiss. His eyes are shifty, blood red, I cannot force them to obey my commands.

Luca laughs loudly, inappropriately. "You're so cute when you're angry." He doesn't let go. Never mind that he's fucking hurting me with that tight grip, I'm getting very uncomfortable now, overly aware of my personal space being invaded.

"Are you drunk?"

"The alcohol was just the starter," Luca smiles, and it all starts to make a little more sense. He must be high on something, and not the mild recreational stuff—or, if it is, he has clearly consumed more than recreational quantities.

"It hardly seems like the time, Luca," I say sternly.

"Now is the perfect time. When the cat's away, the mice can play." He pulls me toward him again, reaching over to try and kiss me. But I shove my hand up into his face, hitting his jaw. The self-defense classes are finally paying off.

"Go to hell, Luca!" I shout, but I still can't get him to release his grip.

"You're being a real bitch, Danica. I thought you wanted this too?" He is annoyed, touching his fingers to his bruised cheek.

"You've lost your mind. All I want is your brother."

"Well, he's not here right now to protect you, is he? I finally get to have you all to myself." Luca grabs both my wrists to hold me down, pinning me against a bookcase with his body. There is nothing sexy about the move. All I feel is panic.

Squirming beneath him, I scream as loudly as I can. The library is tucked away deep within the house, but one of the guards should be around. *Should be.*

But it's not the guards who hear me, it's Alicia. She appears suddenly in the doorway, staring at us confused. Her expression is not what I expect. She looks angry for some reason rather than alarmed.

"What are you doing, Luca?" she asks calmly, too calmly, as she walks toward us. Luca finally lets up and I pull my wrists free from his grip with force.

"Ali..." Luca's face changes, the fury instantly drains from his eyes, replaced by something pathetic. "I was just—"

Alicia doesn't let him finish. She grabs him by the shirt collar, bringing his face inches from hers. "You're fucking this up, Luca. Do you understand that?"

I might as well not be in the room. *What is going on here?* I'm beyond confused.

"I—" Luca tries to protest, but for the second time today, he gets a hand to the face as Alicia punches him.

"Ali, please. It's not what it looks like," he whines, head in his hands.

"Really? Because what it looks like is you chasing after what isn't yours. Again. Can you just stop making everything worse already?" She is clearly on edge. I am still in the dark as to why, but I'm starting to suspect everything isn't as it appears. Alicia looks like she hasn't slept in days.

"I'm not making it worse. I'm fixing it, remember?"

"Does it look *fixed* to you? When are they going to call? You said it would only be one day. That it's just to get the money and then we're good. It's not one day anymore, Luca."

"Not in front of *her*. Shut up, Ali. You're going to get us in trouble." Luca looks panicked, wild eyes darting between Alicia and me.

"What's going on?" I demand but neither of them look at me.

"Nothing. She's just jealous," Luca covers quickly, nervously. He looks fidgety, guilty.

"Yes, yes I am. Because my asshole druggy *boyfriend* can't keep his addictions at bay long enough to follow a simple plan," she hisses through her teeth.

"Your boyfriend—as in *him*?" I ask, looking at Luca, not all that interested in this part of the story. But they clearly know something about Dante's kidnapping.

"I'm not a druggy," Luca says quietly, shoulders drooping. "Please stop."

But his *Ali* has no intention of stopping. She is furious. And fed up.

"No, Luca. This has gone too far. You said Dante wouldn't get hurt. They would just rough him up. I'm starting to realize nothing that comes out of your mouth is ever the truth."

"Where's Dante?" I beg.

"Tell her, Luca. Tell her what you did. You want to be the bad boy. So own up to your shit. Tell Danica how you sold out your own brother to pay off your fucking gambling debts. Tell her about all the cocaine. About how you promised to help them get into Dante's study so they could blackmail the family for more money and you could pay what you owe. How you got me to help you drug Dante's coffee so he'd be defenseless, how I spiked the two guards' food and gave them all food poisoning. Tell her how you promised this would be the last time, this would solve all our problems and we'd finally be free, done with it all. How you were ready to make an honest woman out of me. Tell her the truth for once, Luca." *Hell hath no fury like a woman scorned.*

"You didn't? Luca? Tell me she's making this up." I look at him in desperation, not willing to accept the words that make sense but at the same time, don't.

"No one was supposed to get hurt..." Luca lowers his eyes shamefully.

"Where is he?" I ask for the umpteenth time, this time to someone who might actually have an answer.

"I don't know. They were supposed to just take him and then demand money. I was going to transfer it to them as blackmail money to pay off my debts and they were going to let him go. Easy peasy. But they haven't even called yet..."

"You're an idiot, Luca. They fucking double-crossed you. The same way you double-crossed your own blood. How *could* you?" I clench my fists, listening to my knuckles crack.

"I had no choice. I asked him for help. He didn't help me. He never fucking helps. It is always just about the business. Or you." He glares at me in accusation.

"You gave your brother to the literal fucking enemy, Luca. He doesn't deserve this."

My desperation is quickly turning to anger.

"I called him, you know. He didn't even bother to answer. Last week. Where was he then? When they were beating the shit out of me? They cut off my fucking little toe, Danica! Did Dante even bother to answer his phone? No!" He is pacing around the room. Alicia stands to the side, leaning against the bookcase, arms crossed over her chest—the look of a woman who is done with this shit.

"Is that why you were limping at the banquet?"

"That's beside the point, but yes. He didn't even answer...he never does."

"You know that's not true, Luca. He's always bailing you out of shit."

"Ha! Is that what he tells people?" Luca scoffs. "I—"

He's interrupted by Emilio's unexpected arrival. "Miss Matthews?" the old man asks, trying to read the room.

"Ah, Emilio. Aren't I happy to see you. Could you please help me with something quick?" My voice is calm to the point of being psychotic.

I'm coming, Dante.

Just hold on.

CHAPTER FIFTEEN

CONFESSIONS

Danica...

"**I**s everything okay here, Miss Matthews?" Emilio puts down the tray he's carrying, nodding at Alicia and Luca in greeting. He's moving slower than usual because of the fresh bullet wound in his leg. I tried sending him home but he would not leave my side. *The boss would've wanted me to protect you.*

"Not really, Emilio," I reply, my gaze locked on Luca. It is far from okay. It hasn't been okay since Dante was taken to who-knows-where.

"I brought you some fruit salad, you haven't eaten all day," Emilio explains.

"Thank you, Emilio. That's very considerate of you." I smile through pursed lips, my voice slow and steady, strained. The tension is so thick you can cut it with a butter knife.

"It's my pleasure. What can I assist you with?"

I take my time in answering, weighing up my options carefully before deciding to just go with my first instinct.

"Please pin that asshole to the bookcase." I point at Luca.

"I'm sorry?" Emilio hesitates, looking at me confused.

"Don't." Luca shoots Emilio a glare.

"It seems Luca here knows where Dante is but has been keeping some secrets from us," I reply calmly.

Emilio has him pinned in two seconds flat. "Is this true?" he demands, slamming Luca into the bookcase again. I've never seen Emilio lose his cool but today is an exception—he looks ready to strangle Luca.

"Get your hands off me, Emilio. Do you forget who pays your salary?" Luca laughs, a cocky smirk on his face.

"Not you." Luca's third fist to the face is substantially harder than the first two. It breaks the skin on his cheek and a bruise instantly starts to swell. It makes Luca look even more deranged.

I laugh loudly, manically almost. The sleep deprivation is gnawing at my edges, making me feel dangerously close to losing it. But the satisfaction I feel from seeing Emilio punch Luca in the face brings me great joy. I wish I could hit someone that hard too. Maybe one day.

"I've always wanted to do that," Emilio admits, stretching out his fingers, his knuckles cracking audibly.

Alicia turns to leave, hoping nobody would see her, but I catch a glimpse from the corner of my eye. "Don't even think about it, Alicia. You're as guilty as he is."

"I'm not going down with him. I told you the truth, you—" she starts to bargain but I hold up my hand to silence her, just as I saw Dante do it previously.

"You have nowhere to run, Alicia. So please sit down and be quiet," I instruct, a newfound sense of power coursing through my veins. The accomplice does as she's told, slumping down into one of the oversized armchairs that would be amazing for reading on a rainy day, not today.

She knows she won't get far. The thing about a fortress is that it's as hard to get out as it is to get in. The guards may have been thinned out severely by this week's massacre but the other two have recovered from their food poisoning and are back at their posts.

I turn back to the men.

"Now. Where were we?" I ask Emilio, ignoring Luca's whining.

"I believe Luca was about to tell us where Don Fera is," Emilio says, pressing his forearm into Luca's windpipe, cutting off his air supply.

"Jesus, Emilio…I don't know," Luca gasps, trying to push the bigger man away. But he stands no chance against Emilio. Even injured, he is a formidable force, a force that is in way better shape than Luca's drugged-up, near-delirium body.

"Hold him for me, please, Emilio," I ask politely.

Without warning, I drive my knee into Luca's crotch and he lets out a loud howl when I make contact with his balls. He doubles over but Emilio holds him up.

"Stop lying, Luca. Enough now. Tell me where Dante is."

Luca coughs, the wind knocked out of him completely. I can't believe I just did that but it feels good, right. No more; I'm done being the innocent bystander, the witness, the victim—fuck that. This dickhead better start speaking if he knows what's good for him.

I knee him again and Luca howls in pain, tears flowing freely now. He's a whimpering wreck, held up not by his own legs but Emilio's strength. His red eyes seem to grow even redder as he falls apart, a drugged-up, sleep-deprived disheveled mess. There isn't a single bone in my body that feels any sympathy for Luca Fera. No, the more he comes undone, the angrier I get. *This was all his fault!*

With a single finger, I tilt Luca's chin up, looking him straight in the eye as I grab the knife from the holster around his waist. Nobody stops me. Quick as lighting, I flick open the blade and press it against Luca's pants where my knee had been just moments before, applying just enough pressure for him to feel its shape.

His whimpering stops as Luca sucks in his breath, keeping it inside his chest. Wild eyes darting from side to side, he looks like someone who needs to take a serious break from partying.

"I'm going to ask you one more time, Luca. Just one more time. And you'd better give me a name or I will cut these clean off, understood?" I press the blade against the outline of his cock, moving it lower down to his balls. My mind has a single purpose—bringing Dante home by any means necessary.

Luca gasps. "No...No. Please," he pleads.

"Where is Dante?"

"I don't know!"

"Who knows?!" I press the blade harder, cutting through the fabric of his pants.

"Roberto! Roberto knows. Please stop!" Luca is howling now, crying loudly. It's a distressing scene but nobody moves to help him. He has no lifelines left. "Please..."

"Roberto who?"

"Ricci," Emilio answers for him, easing his grip and letting Luca fall to the ground. "You absolute twat, Luca." Emilio sighs heavily, rubbing his temples. His neutral face is no longer neutral—he looks concerned.

"Is that bad?" I ask.

"It's very bad, Miss Matthews. It's the worst it could be."

"Is Dante okay?"

"I don't know; I hope so. But he's in a lot of danger if the Ricci's have him." He doesn't elaborate.

"We have to go get him!" I insist.

"We need back-up first..." Emilio seems lost in thought.

"There has to be someone we can call."

"I suppose...We are pretty desperate. The Greco family owes us a favor. But I'm not sure Don Fera would want me talking to them," Emilio thinks out loud, considering our options. I sometimes wonder how he kept so many secrets in his head. But I'm grateful for him. I know Dante trusts Emilio with his life, and so do I.

"Whatever we need to do, make it happen, Emilio. Get me Don Greco on the phone please."

"Yes, Ma'am."

"You don't get to call me 'Ma'am,' Emilio." My voice stern but not rude.

"Apologies, Miss Matthews. It won't happen again."

"No problem. What are we going to do with these two though?" I look at Luca on the floor; Alicia is still sitting quietly on the chair, watching it all unfold, waiting for her lot. The one looks more miserable than the other, though both look pretty bleak—they've been caught red-handed in the worst way, like a teenager trying to have a sneaky smoke and accidentally setting the whole forest on fire.

"I'll get Carlo to lock them in the basement until we decide what to do with them. For now, our priority is to get the boss back."

With new-found determination straining my face, I nod. "It absolutely is, no matter what it takes." And I mean it. I'm done being pushed to the sidelines. *Fuck this.*

I just hope we're not too late. *Bloody Luca!* Why couldn't he open his damn mouth earlier already? But what's done is done. The important thing is that we have a lead, even it is doesn't spell anything good.

Dante has to be okay, he just has to. For the first time in my life, the girl who doesn't belong anywhere has somewhere she belongs—in Dante's arms—and I'm not giving that up for anything, definitely not Luca's gambling debts. There is no home without Dante, he is my home.

*My darling boy...*oh god, please let him be okay.

CHAPTER SIXTEEN

LOST

DANTE...

Time passes but I don't know in what measure. Because of the blindfold, there is no telling day from night. There is just darkness—darkness and increasing discomfort.

Sometimes I forget where I am, other times I forget myself. But the one thing I don't ever forget, is my mission to get to Danica. She is the only beacon of light in the darkness, keeping me fighting.

I'm still tied to this fucking chair, held captive by some unknown enemy for some unknown reason. Though I have my suspicions about what's going on.

They are keeping me alive, but barely. Water only. Not enough. Not nearly enough. The thirst in my throat burns almost as brightly as the aching parts of my body. My shoulder wound needs medical attention, it's pulsating, but the kidnappers pay me little mind.

How long have I been here? I don't know. Long enough for me to piss myself a few times over, any request for a bathroom ignored like the rest of my needs. But that is the least of my worries.

I gasp loudly as the cold water hits my face, another glass that would've been better served going down my throat, but instead, I'm desperately trying to lap up whatever drops I can muster, anything to quench this thirst. But the inadequate quantity only makes me more thirsty.

"What do you want?" I cry for the umpteenth time, swallowing hard.

No answer.

The deafening silence makes the thoughts in my head shout faster as the desperation cycles through my body on repeat.

"Why am I here?" I try again, anything to fill the silence.

Finally, another voice sparks like an ember in the darkness, only briefly—fleeting, but tangible.

"*Chiedi a tuo fratello,*" the man who threw the water in my face says simply, closing the door behind him again before I can even formulate any follow-up questions. *Ask your brother.*

Shouting after him, I want more but there are no more answers to be had. Just silence, again. But this time the silence has new information to process, a confirmation of a suspicion I should've accepted as confirmed way earlier. But I didn't want it to be real; I wanted there to be another explanation.

Fucking, Luca. I should've known better than to let him run the dealership. He's failed me so many times, yet I've always given him another chance. He is my little brother after all. I'd wanted to protect him from the evil of the business, from our father—how naive. There was no protecting anyone.

Our father was never one for affection, especially not after our mother died. I'm not sure he'd ever wanted kids. He did it for her. Nobody had planned for the great, cruel boss to be left to raise two young kids alone. So, he didn't. He brought his parents over from Italy to mind us and that was that, we hardly saw him. He was very much of the children-should-be-seen-not-heard generation.

Luca was too young when our mother died—only seven years old. He doesn't really remember what it was like before, or so he says. I had just turned 10. I remember how it felt to be supported, to be loved unconditionally. She had the most beautiful smile...

Our father hadn't taken much interest in Luca. Sure, he'd beat the crap out of him, out of both us, on the regular. Discipline was very important to him. But other than that, he'd let Luca roam free to get up to any mischief he wanted.

I never had that luxury. There was no time to be a kid. One moment I was an awkward 16-year-old with unpredictable acne and dreams of being in a band one day, and the next I stood by silently as I watched my father stab out some guy's eyes for not paying him on time.

Three years of more fucked-up stuff than I care to remember and then it got worse, then it fell on me to be the guy doing the stabbing. There is no way 19 years on this earth was enough to prepare anyone for that role; no age would be. I may have been born a Fera in name but the blood pumping through my veins was always from my mom's side of the family, I suspected.

Not that it made any difference, it was sink-or-swim and if I let us sink, we'd all sink to the bottom of the ocean with weights tied to our bodies. But there was so much to take on, too much. All the responsibility. The business. The debts. The feuds. The endless power struggle with other families...I wanted to run away but I knew that if I did, they'd come for all of us.

Why is this all coming back to me now? Because fucking Luca. I'm trying to make excuses for him again, trying to justify his unjustifiable actions. Maybe I've cut him too much slack? He's not a kid anymore; he can't blame our father for this.

Luca was 16 when our father died, acne-free and whoring his way through the city with no regard for anyone's authority. He didn't give a fuck. He spent his teenage years setting buildings on fire and torturing small animals, forcing me to bail him out (with Emilio by my side) more times than I care to remember. He always promised it would be the last time, that he learned his lesson, that he'd be good now. What a fool I was to ever believe a word that came out of that narcissistic little cunt's mouth.

Luca didn't know how cruel our father really was. I was only five the first time I saw Don Fera Snr. kill a man with his bare hands—our uncle, the head of the family. Although it didn't make sense to me, I'm sure our father had his reasons. Back then, I could never understand what would make a man want to strangle his own brother. But I do now.

"*Stronzo!*" I curse under my breath. Shit.

Although I don't know who my captors are, I have a feeling it's all connected to the missing money somehow, most likely by the thread that is Luca's aura of selfish chaos.

There is nothing I can do though, I can't move. All I can do is hope someone will come for me, but how would they even start to figure out how to find me? I'm usually the one who comes for others, not the one to be saved. Luca sure can't be counted on...

Maybe I should've told Emilio about the stolen money. But I wanted to be sure, wanted to speak to Luca, first. I didn't know who I could trust. Maybe Luigi will come forward now...But I know it is unlikely. He is paid for his silence.

And so time passes. Not quickly, not slowly. Unmeasured.

I black out from time to time, covered in my own urine and blood that has dried to hard flakes I'm desperate to scratch but can't reach.

Part of me still wants to fight, to get to Danica. But a bigger part of me knows there is no fight left in me.

The Knight has failed his Queen.

With every passing moment, I am slipping deeper into the dark abyss that calls me like a siren to an unfortunate sailor.

I don't know how much longer I can remain conscious. The allure of oblivion is strong—not to feel any more pain, not to have my mind run in endless circles that arrive nowhere; I am Sisyphus, pushing that boulder up the hill again and again, only to have it roll down once more, with no hope of salvation.

The last conversation I had with Danica still plays in my mind, repeatedly, more than the events that led to my capture. I don't even care about solving the entire mystery anymore, about finding the *why*. It doesn't matter anymore *why* my own brother sold me out, or *how*...

All that matters is that I failed Danica...even before they captured me. She trusted me with her heart, with her mind, and I treated her no better than those people I promised I was nothing like.

So many regrets...I should've been more patient. I should've communicated better instead of treating her like a child, taking away her free will, and speaking to her like she wasn't the most precious thing in my life (which she is). Shoulda, coulda, woulda...but it was too late; I couldn't undo it.

The worst is not knowing what's happening outside of these walls. Sometimes, I hear people outside, footsteps...but who is to say whether they are real or whether my mind is slowly dipping into insanity. This room could be anywhere.

But I don't know what happened after they took me, how many of my people were killed. I don't know if Danica got away, or whether she's been taken too. I don't know if we'll ever see each other again, alive—that's the one that skewers my heart like a small child watching *Bambi* for the first time.

This is all my fault. Something like this was bound to happen. How naive of me to think I could keep Danica away from the business part, just wrap her up in cotton and keep her safe. It was never in my control. I should've just burned the empire to the ground ages ago, this empire I never asked for and never wanted. What was the point of it if all it ever led to was more death, more hurt?

Around and around, my thoughts swirl in a whirlpool ready to drown me the moment I let go.

The thought of sinking is tempting, oh so tempting. The bliss, the quiet—it would be so easy.

Oh, Danica. I'm sorry, Tesoro.

CHAPTER SEVENTEEN

PREP

DANICA...

The gothic castle Don Greco calls home towers before me like an imposing fortress as I hesitate for only a second before knocking. It's even bigger than the Fera mansion, and built in a completely different style.

But I'm not here to review their architecture; I have important business to handle. With only Emilio by my side, I lift the heavy knocker, announcing our arrival that was surely already announced by the gate guards.

My heart races uncontrollably as I wait for the door to swing open, the ancient-looking butler ushering us into the foyer with a neutral expression.

I can't believe I'm here. Don Greco has been extremely cooperative. As soon as I requested a meeting, he agreed to see me. Who knows what Emilio told him, but it was enough to get us an audience with the boss, and that's all that matters.

I've never spoken to another Don without Dante by my side. And I've definitely never waltzed into such a powerful figure's private home like I'm just popping over for a casual cup of tea, unarmed, unprotected. But no weapon could put me at ease, not in this situation.

What the fuck are you doing, Danica?

You're out of your league.

This is how you die!

The intrusive thoughts ramble through my head as a guard quickly frisks us to ensure we have nothing on us. Every hair on my neck is standing bolt upright, shivers scattered on my skin, but I stand up straight, keeping my head high.

Just get through the next bit, I tell myself, forcing my mind to compartmentalize. One moment at a time. If I think about the big picture, I will lose my nerve, I know I will. But I have to do this, I have to bring my baby-boy home.

Forcing a fake smile on my face, the one I used to wear during my days in the service industry, I put one foot ahead of the other, focusing on the sound of my rhythmic footsteps on the wooden floor. I don't notice the decor, the color of the carpets...nothing. My mind sees only one picture, one face—Dante.

With a single knock, we're permitted into Don Greco's study. It's even bigger than Dante's office, filled with photographs of his smiling family. It's an intimate touch that sticks in my mind long after I forget all the other details of his imposing office. Dante doesn't have any pictures in his office...

My breath threatens to speed up beyond my control as I survey the dimly-lit space, but I force myself to stay calm. Even as I feel the weight of the guards' eyes on me, their fingers likely hovering near triggers.

Despite my nerves, my voice is steady as I explain our dire situation to Don Greco. He looks like any harmless old man, but I know better. He's way older than Dante, maybe in his 70s already, and his fingers are scarred in crisscrossed white lines that I'm sure nobody ever dares ask about.

"The Riccis are a nuisance," the old man sighs when I finish my tale; he seems almost bored with the topic as he pours himself a whiskey from an elegant glass decanter that's probably older than I am. I decline his offer for a drink; I need to stay clear-headed, focused.

From our brief conversation, it's clear nobody likes the Ricci family. "This has gone too far," Don Greco says simply without bothering to elaborate. You don't kidnap a Don without consequences. "It's sleazy and it upsets the natural order." I can't say I disagree, but I don't say anything.

I don't ask why the Grecos owe Dante a favor or why they care enough to help. All that matters is when Don Greco tells his guard, "Get her whatever she needs," he means it. What I need is manpower, and lots of it.

None of the other families want a war; they all have too much at stake. "War is only profitable for arms dealers," Don Greco explains. But I sense there's more to his willingness to help than wanting to avoid a war. There is a tenderness in his voice when he mentions Dante's name. He looks into the distance, his voice softening. "I promised her..." he trails off. I don't press. My mission is to get to Dante, and fast.

As respectfully as I can, I thank the Don and take my leave. Patience is not my strong point—especially not when I'm fearing for the life of the man who has become the most important person in my life.

After leaving the Greco compound, we move swiftly. We find Roberto Ricci at his usual hangout—the brothel on 7th Street. Cunty little fellow, Roberto—no backbone. All he cares about is finishing inside the woman tied to the bed. That and keeping his genitals attached to his body.

The trembling creep spills everything he knows as soon as I threaten him the same way I did Luca. Dante is at a nearby warehouse apparently, hidden under some fake shell company the Riccis use to launder money through. Roberto can't say if Dante is still alive, he doesn't know.

Luca was a fool to trust the Riccis, thinking they'd honor any deal. They don't care about Luca's debt. This isn't about money; it's about power. The Riccis saw a chance to weaken the Feras, and Luca handed them Dante on a silver platter. *Fucking idiot.*

Before leaving the brothel, I smash Roberto's phone under my boot. It won't stop him from warning his family, but it might buy us some time. And time is a valuable commodity right now.

Every minute we waste is a minute closer to Dante's demise, I'm certain. But nobody speaks it out loud. Who would dare?

We prepare quickly, dressing from head to toe in black. Emilio takes me to a massive arsenal in the basement—a hidden stockpile of weapons and holding cells, currently occupied by Luca and Alicia.

The old guard tries to convince me to stay behind. *Don Fera would want you safe*, he argues. But he knows it's futile. I'm going, with or without his consent. The thought of waiting at home, watching the clock, is unbearable. I need to be there, for Dante and for myself.

As some sort of unbalanced compromise, I agree to stay out of the direct action, hiding behind our army of mobsters. More than twenty men in black suits, armed to the teeth, should be enough back-up, right? *Right?*

Reluctantly consenting, Emilio sighs and lets me choose a weapon from the arsenal. I go for the 9mm, familiar with its weight and grip. Tucking it into the holster around my waist, I feel like a Bond-girl supervillain. I hope I won't have to use it, but I can't think about that now. Instead, I focus on Dante's face, his smell, the memory of his arms around me. If it comes to it, my limited gun training will have to be enough.

Now is the time to be strong, to step up and take control. I'm tired of always being scared, of needing to be saved. It's time I learn to fend for myself, especially if I'm serious about building a life with Dante.

Oh Dante. Every bone in my body aches for him. It's near impossible to think of anything else. The need to see his face, to know that he's okay, overrides everything else—even the exhaustion tugging at my edges, the hunger I should feel but don't...

"We need to go, now!" I shout, rallying our army. We've wasted enough time. The night is creeping on, wasting valuable hours of darkness, darkness we need for cover.

Within the hour, everything is set. Our unmarked black vans pull up a block away from the Ricci warehouse that, from the outside, looks like any other storage facility on the road. The Greco vans are indistinguishable from ours and I wonder if everyone shops from the same shady dealers. (I wouldn't be surprised if they did.)

It's now or never.

The element of surprise may be lost, but we have no choice. Sometimes, you have to take back what's yours with brute force.

Hold on, baby, I'm coming for you.

Chapter Eighteen

ATTACK

Danica...

It all happened so quickly, I didn't have time to question my choices. But now, sitting in the van, about to ambush the warehouse that hopefully holds Dante, the weight of my decisions crashes down on me like a ton of bricks.

My heart is pounding in my throat, my hands trembling like they belong to someone else. *Am I actually going through with this?*

But I have to; I have to save Dante. I have never been more certain of anything in my life.

This is crazy! My current reality is a long way from my suburban upbringing that only prepared me for a life of ignorance. But none of that matters now. Without Dante, I could never be safe again. No matter how you look at it,

I am not the one risking it all; everything has already been put at risk.

On high alert, I look around me for the umpteenth time, trying to relax my tense shoulders but they refuse to budge. Emilio is beside me, in the driver's seat, all dressed in black—same as me, as all of us. It is almost time to move out. *Oh god, I hope we're not too late.*

Carlo and another guard I should remember the name of but don't are sitting in the backseat. Behind us, four more unmarked black vans stand ready in the shadows on the side of the road. The tree-lined streets provide the perfect cover, even if we had to park a block away just to be safe.

"Are you ready, Miss Matthews?" Emilio asks, brows locked in an intense look that has been on his face since we left the library. I'm glad he's the one in control, but I still wish I was following Dante into battle instead. Dante always makes me feel calm, safe. But I don't feel either of those things now.

Staring straight ahead, I nod. I'm not ready yet but I know it's now or never. Dante's coming home with us, that's my sole mission. Nothing else exists. How could it without him? What kind of Domme fails to protect their sub?

I wait as the men file out of the vans as they head towards the warehouse, keeping to the shadows, staying low. As promised, I'm somewhere near the back with three of them behind me to fend off any surprise attacks.

As we cover the distance between us and the nondescript warehouse, I push my nervousness back, forcing my mind to focus. Part of me worries that Dante isn't here, that it is all a trap, but it's the only lead we have.

This is crazy! This doesn't feel real. Am I actually creeping towards a mob family's warehouse with a gun strapped to my body?

Quiet!

Focus, Danica.

This is not the time for thinking, this is the time for action.

Watch your feet.

Counting my breathes, I reach ten before starting over. Treading lightly, I move forward like a cat, each step a delicate balance between stealth and speed. Perhaps doing all those squats with Emilio was worth it. I like how my body moves. *Maybe I'll add some weights next time—*

We reach the clearing where the shadows stop, the part where we're fully exposed in the bright glow of the street light, and my mind goes quiet, listening, watching for hidden threats. It's pure instinct. I may not have been born into a crime family, but I've by no means lived a sheltered life. Watching for threats is second nature.

This time I don't fawn in the face of danger. No, I keep my head low and run toward a warehouse full of mobsters.

There are two guards at the gate but they are dead before they even see us coming. I don't even flinch at the sound of the gunfire anymore, though I'm grateful for the silencers to keep my ears from ringing like a bitch.

We burst through the gate without bothering to try and be quiet, filing into the premises in double lines as chaos ensues around us.

They know we're here. Shots fly past me in every direction, and I keep low like Emilio told me to, hoping it's enough. *What the fuck are you doing, Danica?* the voice in my head chides but I refuse to give it any airtime. There is no turning around now.

Breathe, Danica.

The short distance between the external gate and the warehouse building feels like a marathon. We're exposed, clear targets in the open stretch, but we move quickly, reaching the building's entrance with only one casualty.

Despite the temptation, I don't look back; I never do. Hunched low, eyes locked on the men in black ahead, we barge through the glass door, shattering it with ease.

It was easy up to this point. Too easy. I suddenly realize why. A wall of armed men meets us in the reception area, waiting, ready, guns cocked and ready.

Fuck!

The human shields on either side of me push forward, taking out the Ricci guards faster than they can hit us. What type of warehouse it is, is still not clear. We seem to be in the office side of it; I've seen no actual products or storage pallets. It's probably just a warehouse on paper; what really happens here, nobody but the Riccis know.

Though I know I should stay close to the group, stay protected, the need to find Dante overrides all logic. He has to be here, behind one of the many doors lining the corridor.

Like a single unit, we move through the maze of hallways. The mission is to clear the guards first, then find Dante—I know that—but my need to find him overrides the logic of this simple plan. I can't shake the fear that they will shoot my tattooed god when they realize the building is under attack.

I slow my pace, sidestepping to let another guard pass. He's too focused on the mission to notice me. Gradually, I make my way closer to the back of the group.

The final man in line is distracted by the gunfire happening on the front line, he doesn't notice me, or if he does, he doesn't register who I am. We all look similar in our black gear.

Finally, I'm at the back. There is nobody behind me now. Keeping my back against the wall, I duck into the first room on the left. Immediate disappointment sinks into my belly as soon as the light flickers on—the room is empty. It's just some storage space.

Quickly, I exit again, looking both ways before darting across the hall to the opposite door. It's empty, as are the next two doors. *What if they've moved him somewhere else?*

Anxious to find my good boy, I crawl from room to room, keeping low, as our ambush pushes deeper into the facility. The Riccis have plenty of guns but not plenty of men from what I can tell, but it's hard to gauge from this far back.

There's an orange door coming up on my right. From what I can tell, it's an engine room of some sort. Probably for the building's air conditioning. I straighten as I enter, reaching for the light switch, but a sudden, sharp pain in my arm stops me.

I scream as the knife sinks into my flesh. *Oh god, it hurts!* I struggle to push the hidden attacker away, but I can't see a thing. Blood runs down my arm; the cut is deep. Adrenaline floods my veins, taking over.

With great effort, I flick the switch with my other hand, just in time to see the masked man lunging again, knife in hand.

Hesitating, I pull the 9mm from its holster, a practiced motion. *Can I actually shoot someone?*

But it's not my shot that sends the attacker to the floor; it comes from behind me. Relief washes over me instantly.

"You have to be careful, Miss Matthews," Emilio urges, his large figure blocking the door.

Fuck. That was close, too close. I don't know if I could've pulled the trigger but it doesn't matter right now.

Where's Dante?

Chapter Nineteen

PROTECTOR

Dante...

The darkness in my mind is pierced by a commotion outside. It can't be a dream, it's too loud. *But what if it is?*

By now, I am just drifting in and out of consciousness, uncertain whether any time is passing or not. My blindfold is still firmly in place, blocking out the room.

I have no idea what's going on. My world has been confined to this uncomfortable chair for what feels like ages, but I suspect it has only been a few days. I can't feel my limbs anymore though—the rough rope ties are too tight.

My heart beats faster as the sounds draw closer.

I'd know that voice anywhere. It can't be though.

"I said—let him go!" the voice repeats, louder this time; closer.

Danica!

It must be a fever dream. She can't be here. My desperate longing has materialized her in this cold, dark room. *Am I finally losing it?*

What I won't give for it to be Danica for real. But she can't be here, it is too dangerous. *Why would she be here?*

The noise outside doesn't die down or fade like the dream I suspect it of being. I hear more shouting in Italian, lots of shuffling, a struggle. For a moment I'm almost sure I hear Emilio.

A gunshot. It brings my drifting mind back to the present.

It's no dream. The sound of the gunshot is unmistakable, and it came from right outside the door.

There is another shot. And another.

Have they come for me? I don't want to get my hopes up.

The door opens and I hear heavy footsteps rushing in towards me. They sound like the same ones that always came in, the ones that threw water in my face and refused to give me any more info.

This is it, I think. *This is how I go. Oh god.*

"If you touch him I will fucking end you!" The voice is loud and clear, unmistakable. *Danica!*

The energy in the room shifts suddenly. The water guy must be close, I feel a tug on my ropes. This is not good.

The next gunshot is very close, too close. The perpetrator screams, collapsing at my feet, his hand brushing against my ankle. I wish I could see, but all I can do is hold my breath, hoping this is real, and if it is, that the right person wins. I'm too weak to help.

"I don't like to be disobeyed, you asshole! I warned you." It *is* Danica. And she sounds furious. It must be a dream. She hates guns. Sure, I forced her to learn how to use one but under great protest. She refused to carry one, even when I insisted.

"You can thank your lucky stars it was just your leg, douchebag," the voice booms.

The man on the floor is pleading for his life in Italian, but I know Danica doesn't understand nor would she care if she could.

More gunshots ring outside, so many more. It's making my ears hurt but I can't do anything to cover them. My body is one with this chair. So, I just wait in the dark and hope nothing happens to Danica. I am powerless to defend her; I can't even defend myself.

And then it goes quiet, eerily so.

"Danica?" I breathe, my voice barely a whisper. *It can't be her, right?*

But it *is* her. I know that scent anywhere, the feeling of her proximity. My body instantly reacts, melting into the chair with relief.

"Dante! It's okay, darling, you're safe now," Danica replies as her delicate hands pull the blindfold from my face.

But I can't see anything. Even the dim light in the room is too much for my sensitive eyes accustomed to only darkness.

"You came for me." I'm in utter disbelief.

"Of course I came for you, baby. I will always protect you."

She kisses my forehead, arms wrapping around me. Winching from the pain in my shoulder, I focus on the part that feels good, the part where I am in Danica's arms again.

I feel like crying, I'm so relieved—not just to be saved, but to feel her near me again. Being away from her was agony. Not only that, I didn't want her last memory of me to be throwing her out of the house.

"I'm so sorry," I say weakly, hearing the tears swelling in my voice.

"It's okay, baby. You did what you had to." She presses her forehead against mine.

I think I am crying but I don't know. My senses are flooded with Danica. It's almost too much to bear.

My eyes slowly adjust to the harsh light and I take in her beautiful face through the haze. She looks so different; transformed. Dressed all in black, hair tied back, thick boots—my Queen looks ready for war. I never imagined seeing her like this, my own G.I. Jane to the rescue.

"You have never looked more beautiful," I tell her, my voice cracking. It's true.

A sad smile tugs at the corners of her lips. "I wish I could say the same." Her grin is fleeting, replaced by a look of deep concern as she gently touches my cheek. Her fingers are warm against my cold, clammy skin. I can't fathom what she sees—a broken, battered shell of the person I once was. How can she still touch me with such tenderness, given the state I'm in?

Behind her, Emilio and other black-clad figures come into focus. I recognize some of my men but the others are unfamiliar. Emilio's limping a tad but it does little to make him look less threatening. His presence is commanding and authoritative—like in the old days when my father used to send us on debt-collecting duties together.

"*Don mio*." He smiles, nodding in my direction respectfully without interrupting Danica.

"Thanks for rescuing me," I tell him.

"You should thank Miss Matthews, boss."

"Oh trust me, I will. I'll spend the rest of my life thanking her." I rest my head on her chest, closing my eyes for a moment.

"Sometimes the Queen must save her Knight too, you know." Danica kisses my hair. "Let's get you out of these ties, baby."

Please don't let this be a dream.

CHAPTER TWENTY

QUEEN

DANICA...

"**E**veryone, out!" I shout, the adrenaline still pumping through my veins. Nobody dares question the authority in my voice.

Emilio ushers the men out of the room, closing the door behind him to give us a moment of privacy. I know he's guarding the door, just like he does when we're at home.

Carelessly, I drop my gun on the ground. It makes a clinking sound as the metal hits the bare cement that looks like it hasn't seen a mop in a decade. The rest of the room doesn't look much better; the damp patches on the wall spread out like a grotesque Rorschach test. The place is definitely giving *Saw* vibes.

Without the burden of the gun, I'm free to cradle Dante's face with both hands. Tears are trailing down his cheek, cutting through the dried blood and leaving pale trails in their wake. I kiss them away, indifferent to the dirt and gore. His eyes meet mine and for an eternity we just stare at each other. So much to say, but no words seem appropriate, or enough.

With a quick, decisive motion, I pull the knife from my belt and start cutting through the ropes binding Dante's bruised body. My hand falters, the fresh cut on my arm throbbing, but I push through, my focus unwavering.

Dante is a shadow of his usual self. His pants are ripped, his feet bare and bloodied. My heart breaks to see him this hurt, so weak. Protective rage courses through me like wildfire.

But he's alive. That's the most important part.

Still, I'm furious, like a lioness whose cub has been threatened. *How fucking dare they?* How dare any of them? *Fucking Luca.*

After Emilio saved me in the control room, I wasn't stupid enough to navigate the rest of the rooms alone. I made sure to take one of the guards for cover as we barged into the empty store rooms one by one.

The Ricci's men never stood a chance. We were too powerful with the Greco's army behind us too. I don't think they were expecting that. *Thank you, Emilio!*

With every yard we gained, pushing the men back and back until their numbers dwindled to single digits, another door came within reach. But none of them were hiding Dante.

By the time we got to the back of the facility, the Ricci men had scattered, realizing the futility of their defense against our sizable army. I was quickly losing hope of finding Dante here. *We're too late.*

And then, suddenly, just another unmarked door in an unmarked corridor, there he was! Dante. Alive. But oh god, he looked wrecked.

There was no time to think, no time for pity. Some asshole was running towards Dante faster than I could close the distance between us.

This time I didn't hesitate to pull the trigger.

Thank fuck I hit my target. I didn't want to kill anyone, just stop the guy. Luckily my aim wasn't too bad and I got him without accidentally shooting Dante in the process—that was my biggest fear.

Now that the threat has been removed, I can focus on Dante. *Shit, his shoulder looks really bad.* The Doctor better be ready to perform some miracles.

"Can you move?" I ask once the cut ropes are on the floor.

"I don't know," Dante croaks, trying to put some weight on his legs. But he collapses again almost instantly. Who knows how long he's been stuck in that position, his massive frame bent awkwardly around the chair.

Struggling to keep my balance, I hoist him up, ignoring the throbbing pain radiating from my wounded arm. The temptation to call in Emilio for assistance is great, but I'm determined to get by on my own. I don't want anyone touching Dante but me. *He's mine!*

Dante grips the back of a chair to steady himself, his other hand clutching my shoulder. Together, we manage to get him into some semblance of an upright position. His steps are shaky, each one a monumental effort, but he pushes through. He makes it two steps before collapsing onto an old table near the wall, oblivious to the spiderwebs festooning the corners.

The sight of him struggling breaks my heart, but it also fuels my determination.

"My legs need to wake up..." Dante's words are slow, like it's taking a lot of effort to form them.

"It's okay baby, take your time." I wrap my arms around him, hugging him to me despite the sharp jab of pain it sends surging through my arm.

Reaching up, I kiss him deeply, hungrily—feral almost. The rush of emotion is instant. Fuck how vile he smells; I'm just relieved to be back in his arms where I belong.

I never knew I could miss that feeling so much. It's only been a few days but the fear of losing it all, makes it feel so much sweeter.

Dante's cock twitches between our hugging bodies, and I grin, gently petting his growing erection over his torn pants.

"Well, well, well—what do we have here?"

"I missed you," he says, still holding me close.

I look up into Dante's hollow eyes, at his broken face, and kiss him again, devouring his lips lustfully, sloppily.

I missed you doesn't even begin to cover it.

All the emotions—the overwhelming panic and fear of the past few days—is finally freed from the box I've held shut firmly to get me through this mission. *Holy fuck!*

Every sense is on high alert, pulsing with adrenaline; my heart rate still hasn't slowed down.

Dante could've died, *I* could've died. This is crazy! *What am I even doing here?*

But I know what I'm doing here, I'm protecting my good boy, just like I promised him I would so many times.

"Don't ever leave me again," I tell Dante, lacing my fingers through his. Despite the situation, our injuries, I still have an insane urge to pin him on the table and fuck him right here, right now. But there's no time—we need to get out of here—so I resist the desire to make him show me his hard cock; to show me how much he missed me.

Dante kisses my fingers. "I won't ever leave you again, *Tesoro*. You are my everything."

At first, the words catch me off-guard but the sincerity in Dante's eyes quickly soften any reservations I may have had. He means it.

I kiss him one more time, putting my hand on his heart.

"Let's go home, baby boy. You need a bath."

He probably needs a lot more...

CHAPTER TWENTY-ONE

AFTERMATH

DANICA...

We are not out of the woods, not even close. Dante keeps drifting in and out of consciousness as Carlo speeds through backroads to get us home. Emilio already called The Doctor, he'll meet us there.

"Come on, baby, stay with me," I tell Dante, kissing his too-hot forehead. There is nothing I can do to help the situation, still, I nag Carlo insistently to *drive fucking faster already!*

The Doctor is already waiting when we get home, assuring us that there is nothing to worry about, though I'm plenty worried. With a warm cloth, I bathe Dante's face while The Doctor assesses the damage: some cracked ribs, and that nasty gunshot wound in his shoulder.

"He is lucky, there is no damage to his internal organs and the bullet went straight through," Emilio translates for me as the doctor prepares to clean out the shoulder wound and stitch it up.

"*Lucky* would've been not getting fucking kidnapped in the first place, I'd say," I mumble, but Emilio wisely doesn't translate.

It's too gross, I can't watch as the doctor drives the needle through Dante's skin. Dante doesn't even groan much, just takes it. The little energy he had when I first untied him from that chair has long since dissipated after our hurried exit from the Ricci warehouse.

The doctor hands me a bottle of antibiotics with Emilio translating the instructions of three times a day, with meals.

"Is that all?"

"Is there anything else, Miss Matthews?" Emilio asks as The Doctor moves on to fixing up my arm, a considerably less infected-looking wound than Dante's.

"Will he be okay though?" I look over to Dante, fast asleep in the bed. His color is off completely; he doesn't look like himself.

"He just needs to rest, Miss Matthews."

I should've called bullshit. But for two days, I let them tell me it will be fine as I impatiently wait for Dante to get better, to come back to me. Somehow, this is not quite the happy reunion I had imagined. I am glad to have Dante home, but he looks worse now than when we found him.

Try as I might, I can't get him to eat anything without throwing it up again, and the meds have done fuck all to improve the situation. He hardly even has the strength or awareness to recognize me most of the time, and his breathing remains irregular, his heartbeat pounding against my ear whenever I put my head on his chest. *It's fine, Miss Matthews.* Except it's not.

If only I paid closer attention—it's Emilio who notices the expiry date on the antibiotics first. They are more than a year past their effective date. *Fuck!* Shady shit from a shady doctor. "Get him in the car!" I tell Emilio, throwing the blankets off Dante in a hurry. He is sweaty from the fever that refuses to break its grip on him, his complexion as ashen as the grey skies outside.

"Miss Matthews, The Doctor is on his way." Emilio tries to keep me calm, but I can see the worry on his face as he regards Dante's desperate condition.

"No, fuck that guy. Dante needs real help. Get him in the car."

"It doesn't work like that, Miss Matthews. This will complicate matters."

"Dante dying will complicate matters, now get that fucking car, Emilio. I am not asking again!" I know I'm being rude, but I'll seek Emilio's forgiveness later. There will be no forgiveness for anyone if Dante dies on me now. "Please," I add, my voice pleading.

Emilio takes one more look at Dante and nods, calling in some guards to help carry Dante to the car, body limp hanging between them—dead weight. *Oh god, hold on!*

"Get out!" I tell Carlo when I reach the car already waiting in the driveway. He looks to Emilio for direction but the older man just nods and lets me take the driver's seat, adjusting the seat so I can reach the pedals.

It probably would've made more sense to take one of them with me but I don't trust anyone to take me where I need to go. Fuck their secrets and shady doctors, there is only one person I trust with my life.

So, I take Dante to my childhood GP, Doctor Carter—she's been our family doctor since before I was even born, and always treated me with kindness. I know she has many questions but she doesn't ask them. The desperation on my face is as obvious as the vague lies I tell her to spin a cover story. My boyfriend got into a fight, we thought the wound would heal okay.

Skipping past the line of waiting patients, Doctor Carter checks Dante into the hospital herself, sending me to wait in the stupid reception room with the too-white walls and gardening magazines that have been read to shreds.

There are no forms to fill in. Emilio has promised to smooth it all over on the admin side, ensuring the police don't get involved. I know it won't be easy, but Dante getting better is more important than fucking paperwork.

After the rush of the drive—darting through traffic like a real-life game of *Grand Theft Auto* (minus the injury of innocent civilians)—the room feels too quiet, pointless. I pace up and down, restless.

There's only one person I want to see but Doctor Carter tells me that I can't see him yet, she first needs to redo Dante's stitches and clean out the wound properly.

She comes out to tell me that a piece of flesh is already rotten and she has to cut it out. The infection was poisoning his body, he had septicemia. I don't know if it's dangerous but she said it's very. *Fuck, fuck, fuck.*

"Do what you have to," I tell her, continuing my pacing as soon as the doctor disappears beyond the grey swinging doors again.

Googling septicemia does little to put me at ease, it freaks me out even more. *This is bad, shit.*

The doctor's last recommendation is for me to call someone, for me. For a moment I pause, uncertain whether my message will be appropriate, but I send it anyway. There is nobody else I can think to contact.

Despite bracing for certain rejection, they reply with *on my way*.

When Doctor Carter finally lets me into the room where they're keeping Dante, I collapse into the chair beside his bed, burying my head in my hands. *Oh, god!*

He looks like shit, so weak, so pale—like an empty vessel. Various tubes run from his body as the machine steadily beeps beside the bed like I'm on some episode of *Grey's Anatomy*. But it's not TV, it's real life, it's Dante. It breaks me to see him like this.

"Is he going to be okay?" I ask, moving my chair closer so I can hold Dante's hand.

"His body has suffered a lot of trauma, but he should hopefully recover. It's too soon to say with certainty. His organs are still unaffected, that's the good news. You brought him in on time, barely, but on time. Now, all we can do is wait for the medicine to do its thing and for his body to heal. "

With my head hanging low, I let out a strained sigh, fighting back exhausted tears.

"Danica, what have you gotten yourself into?" The doctor puts a hand on my shoulder.

"I can handle it."

"Danica…"

"No, please. Not now."

"Okay. Try and get some rest," the doctor tells me as she exits, and I just nod, no intention of listening to her advice.

When Adira shows up 27 minutes later, I am eternally grateful to see the curly-haired Goddess come toward me with open arms, hugging me close like we are old friends. She was the only person I could think to call, the only one who wouldn't ask too many questions I couldn't (or wouldn't) answer.

"Oh, Danica, darling," is all she says, but it's enough for me to let go, collapsing in emotion that refuses to be repressed any longer.

"I don't want to be alone," I tell her, soaking Adira's shirt with all the tears I've been holding back.

"It's okay, I'm here for you." She sits down on the couch and motions for me to join her. Without saying anything else, I lay my head on her lap, curling myself up into a little ball, my body wrapped around hers.

"He can't die, please, please…I love him, Adira. I really love him."

"I know, baby, I know."

As Adira strokes my hair, I finally allow myself to drift into a restless sleep riddled with nightmares I only remember the feeling but not the content of later.

She keeps telling me it will be okay, and I sincerely hope there is some truth to her prophecy.

It doesn't feel okay.

CHAPTER TWENTY-TWO

REVIVAL

DANTE...

I drift in and out of consciousness, ripped from one world to the other, in no particular rhythm or routine. Sometimes I'm in the hospital, Danica by my side, her familiar scent keeping me calm...other times, I'm still tied to a chair in that dark room, certain my life is about to end.

The only constant is the pain in my body, the sheer stubbornness of my limbs as they refuse to obey my commands. I want to reach out to Danica, to tell her I'm happy to see her, to have her here, but I don't know if I ever say those words out loud. It's all a blur.

The dreams are vivid, so, so real. I know it's all in my mind, but sometimes I see them so clearly, like they're right here.

In my dreams, I'm a teenager again, running through the shiny streets of Vegas, laughing. That face, it's been so long since I've seen (or even thought of) that face, but it's unmistakably them. It's a face I've tried to forget for so many years, but it haunts me in my delirium, taunting me with the future I could never have.

We can't do this, I tell them in my dream. *Tell me you don't want this too*. I can't, even in my dream I can't lie to those beautiful amber eyes.

And just like that, they're gone again, replaced by Elena's kind face, smiling at me with the wind in her hair. But it all soon turns to carnage, like it always does.

Every time the dreams dissipate, it's only Danica's face who remains. I try to smile at her, but my eyes remain closed. Maybe tomorrow.

Finally, after a period of time still unknown to me, the shaky world stabilizes and I manage to squeeze Danica's hand, real Danica, not dream Danica.

"Dante!" She touches my cheek affectionately, her eyes red and tear-stained.

I try to speak but my throat is too dry, but I manage a smile.

"Oh, my baby. Please stay with me." Danica takes my hand and I use all the strength I have to squeeze her fingers again.

It gets easier after that, I stay with her longer. Finally, I manage more than word, later—a sentence. Time is still a blur but reality is starting to settle a bit more. I stop fearing that I'll just drop away into dreamland never to come back again.

Sometimes Emilio is there too. We sit in silence as he does Sudukos in a little A5 book that Danica bought him. Adira comes too. I'm surprised to see her but happy that Danica has someone to support her. Luca doesn't come, of course, but I don't even ask about him, not yet.

Danica refuses to leave my side. I tell her to go home, to rest, but my Queen is nothing if not stubborn. She sits beside my bed with the books and magazines scattered around the room like it's a library and not a hospital room.

At least it's a private room. It's definitely not ideal but Emilio assured me that everything is taken care of; there will be no questions. The one benefit of the many favors due to the Fera dynasty in this town, over three generations of favors, is that there is always someone willing to look the other way, to make things go away. And if not, cold, hard cash helps for the rest.

I don't ask for the details, I don't need them. Emilio knows what he's doing and I trust him fully.

Every day, I whine that I want to go home, recover in my own bed. But every day the stocky nurse with the permed red hair tells me *not yet.*

At least I'm getting stronger, slowly.

It's a Tuesday when Danica makes me scoot over in the tiny bed to make space for her. Keeping her eyes on me, she pulls the curtain shut around us, shielding us with its flimsy privacy.

The bed is hardly big enough for me, let alone both of us, but I don't mind. I miss her body against mine, her warmth; the way her skin feels against mine.

The effect is instant arousal, I can't even hide it—much to Danica's amusement. She wraps her fingers around my untimely erection tenting under the thin green hospital blanket. "Someone is excited."

"I can't help it." I manage a smile, groaning as Danica teases the blood to my cock, fingers teasing my hardness like it was just another normal day in my office.

Even now, with my body broken and my energy levels on reserve, nothing burns brighter than my need for her. When tied to that cold chair in the Ricci warehouse, I didn't think I'd ever get to feel her touch again. The relief is almost tangible.

Despite the aggravating pain in my shoulder, I hold her tightly, breathing her in. Seeing her like that—so fearless, commanding an entire army—I have never seen anything sexier in my life before! Who knew being rescued would be such a turn-on?

I know my body needs many things to stay alive right now. But the primal urge to devour her whole overrides all other needs.

Danica kisses me desperately, chewing my broken lip as she sucks the air right out of my lungs, hand still resting on my cock.

Like an animal, I groan. I want to answer her question but words fail me. All the blood in my body has drained to the hard flesh beneath her hands.

"I need you inside me," she breathes in my neck, affecting me in ways words cannot describe. *Dio mio!*

I'm so painfully hard. The hunger inside had been replaced by a hunger only for her skin against mine. "Please." My plea is barely audible.

Danica moves her hand away from my cock. "Show me how much you want me." We both know what she's asking.

Despite my desperation, the task is harder than I anticipated. The space is way too small to maneuver with ease, especially with only one good arm, but I know the reward will be worth it.

Finally, I manage to pull my cock out from under the stupid hospital frock that ties in the back. It stands proud and erect, ready.

"Such a good boy," Danica whispers, taking my erection in both hands. Shivers run up my spine as she palms me, slowly at first, and then not-so-slowly. "I love seeing how hard you are for me..."

I grunt, my words lost in the euphoria of the pleasure building in my groin. It's been more than two weeks since I came—not since that morning I woke up still inside her, the morning after the auction...the day it all went to shit.

But I don't want to think about that day anymore. What matters is that I'm here, and that Danica is okay.

She doesn't let me finish, of course not. Even in my broken state, my Queen doesn't have mercy. It somehow makes me feel less broken; she's treating me as she usually would.

"Hold that thought," she tells me as she jumps off the bed with agility I only dream of in my bed-ridden state. As seductively as one can in hospital fluorescent lighting, she kicks off her shoes and sweatpants, stripping only her bottom bare. *Fuck, I've missed that perfect ass.*

"Don't move, baby." Danica climbs back onto the bed, planting a knee on either side of my waist. Careful not to touch my shoulder, she lowers herself onto my cock.

Oh god, she is so wet. I bite down hard to trap a primal cry from roaring from my lips as my Queen grinds down on my dick, slowly at first.

The world around us disappears; I don't even feel the aching that has pained me for so long, all I feel is her. Delirious with lust but fully cognizant (for once), I'm lost in the depths of her desire, of mine.

"No coming without permission," Danica hisses at me, staring deep into my eyes. Oh, how I've missed those words.

"Yes, Mistress," I moan, pulling her hair loose from its messy bun. It falls wildly around her face.

"I've been so empty..." Danica gasps as she rocks her hips into mine, the bed creaking beneath us. Someone could open that curtain at any moment! But Danica doesn't let that slow her down. Keeping her balance through some miracle, she reaches for her clit, rubbing it fiercely in tandem with her hips.

I'm bewitched, lost in the essence of Danica as she ravishes my body like the savage I look and feel like, fucking me until I cry her name in a desperate whisper, pleading with tears in my eyes for her to let me come.

And when she does, when she finally gives me permission, I explode inside her, everything I've pent up over the past few days releasing in a mighty climax that threatens to rip my tired body apart.

Although I can't see it on her face, I feel it as she clenches around me; Danica comes seconds later, our fluids mixing in an extended climax, a complete and beautiful mess.

Panting as heavily as I am, she lies her head down against my heart, and I gather her in my good arm, hugging her tight, still inside her. Her body heaves up and down with my chest as I try to bring my heart rate down.

"Don't you ever fucking leave me again," Danica threatens in a light-hearted tone as she lazily traces her nails over my chest, tugging at my chest hairs as she's done so many times before.

I smile, kissing the side of her head.

"No, Ma'am. Never."

"There's my good boy."

EPILOGUE

Two Months Later...

Chapter Twenty-Three

FOREVER

Danica...

Dante awkwardly models his new outfit for me, and I nearly fall off the bed, uncontrollable laughter ripping through me. It's so...*different!*

The sight of him in the gaudy ensemble, a pair of neon green shorts and a matching tank top adorned with tropical prints, is both endearing and hilarious.

"I look ridiculous," Dante grumbles, stretching his muscular arms out to display the look fully as he turns around for my benefit. The shorts cling to his well-built frame, and the tank top's loud patterns clash with his usually stoic demeanor. He's smiling though, so I know he's just pretending to be grumpy.

"Yes, baby, you absolutely do. But I love it." I blow him a kiss. "Now show me the Hawaiian shirt."

"I have never owned clothes like this," Dante complains as he digs out the bright yellow shirt from one of the many shopping bags we brought back after this morning's spree. The shirt is a vivid explosion of sunflowers and pineapples, a far cry from his usual dark and subdued wardrobe.

Nothing Dante owned was suitable for our island vacation, but I hadn't noticed until we'd already arrived in Greece. Already halfway out the door, I was donned in my favorite classic one-piece and ready for the ocean. Meanwhile, Dante stood around awkwardly in his jeans and a black t-shirt—his idea of "beach casual."

So, I put on a dress and dragged him to the shop for more *appropriate* attire. Unfortunately for him, it was only a small store and their limited selection had little to offer a man of his size. Now poor Dante has to make do with an overly brightly colored assortment of shorts and vests, much to my amusement (and his horror).

As he pulls on the Hawaiian shirt, the fabric drapes awkwardly over his broad shoulders. The bright yellow material is almost blinding, and the floral print is cheerful to the point of absurdity. He looks like walking sunshine, and I can't help but burst into giggles again. Dante's expression softens as he catches my eye, and he finally joins in the laughter, the sound deep and rumbling.

"Who wears this kind of shit?" Dante asks, inspecting himself in the mirror.

Slipping in under his arm, I hug him sideways, regarding the reflection in the mirror in more detail. It doesn't look like Dante at all, maybe a different Dante.

"People who have lives and go on holiday," I answer his rhetorical question.

"That doesn't sound like me."

"It does now. This is our new life."

"I wish we could just leave for good. Just pack up and move somewhere else. Anywhere. I don't want to risk losing this." Dante sighs, kissing the top of my head.

"We can't leave, darling. You know that. Nobody leaves this business alive, you always tell me. Besides, I don't want to leave. It's my home. My family is there, my friends. I don't want to put them at risk. You know this would never end if we just left. Let's sort this shit out between the families and make peace once and for all."

"You're far too optimistic. But you are right. It can't go on like this."

"Besides, we need to be there for Luca. He's going to have a tough time when he comes out of rehab."

"He can go to hell, he—" Dante clenches his fists, anger flashing across his face.

"He's all you have. We'll look after him." My voice is soothing, patient, as I rest my hand on his chest.

"He doesn't deserve it."

"No, but we'll do it anyway. It's what your mother would have wanted."

Dante's face softens, and he unclenches his fists. "You really haven't chosen an easy life when you picked me, have you?"

"No, but I wouldn't want it any other way, *Tesoro*."

"Forever at your service, my Queen." Dante picks up my hand and kisses it, one finger at a time. "Whatever you want."

"Well, now that you mention it. There *is* something I want..." A grin spreads over my face.

"Don't say it."

"I've been dying to all day."

"I know. Don't," he threatens, but I can see a smile starting to form around the corner of his mouth.

"You know you can't stop me." I stick my tongue out at Dante like an insolent child, teasing him.

Dante sighs, feigning annoyance. "Fine. Just do it. I'm impressed you got this far without mentioning it."

"It's because I whispered it to you in your sleep before you woke up. So many times." I smile victoriously.

Dante shakes his head, smiling unreservedly now. "You're an absolutely crazy woman, you know that right?"

"But you love me anyway?"

Dante just laughs and doesn't reply.

"Happy birthday, baby." I stand on my tippy-toes and pull him closer for a kiss. His lips moved against mine with a hunger that mirrored my own, igniting a fire that burned deep within me. There was just something about Dante's kiss, the way it unlocked my body like no other key in existence.

"How many times do I have to tell you I don't do birthdays?" Dante whispers when we finally part, still holding me close.

"All the times. You still came on this trip, didn't you?"

"You were very persuasive. Still, I can't believe I let you drag me all the way to Greece."

"It's beautiful though. Look at all this." I gesture to the magnificent room around us, the beautiful palms and ocean view through the wide doors of our honeymoon suite balcony. No expense was spared—the Fera way.

"Sure, the view's not bad," Dante admits, pulling me in for another quick kiss. "Thank you for insisting."

I did more than insist, I booked the flights and the accommodation before even telling him. After that hellish two-week period in the hospital, the blur of the days that followed as Dante slowly recovered, we needed this, we *deserved* this.

"So, I got you two things for your birthday..." I wink.

"Danica!" he scolds.

"I know, I know. I promised no presents. But trust me, you're going to like this. One will be annoying to get home but the other one...Hmm..." I tease, disappearing to the bedroom to retrieve the gifts before Dante can protest any further.

When I return, he's seated in the large leather armchair by the balcony door, watching me intently.

"Firstly, for your Zen collection." I pull a small, elegant bonsai tree from behind my back and hand it to him. "I know how much you like gardening."

Dante smiles. "Is this because of my temper?"

"I'm not saying that. But I would like to stop finding those little Zen garden rocks on the floor, hey?" My voice is playful, the wink at the end ensuring he knows I'm just teasing.

"Fair enough. Thank you. It's very thoughtful."

"And then, there's this..." I reveal my other hand from behind my back and hand him the A4-sized black metal case. It has no writing, no indication of its contents, just a simple golden bow on the top.

"What is this?" Dante asks, immediately opening the lid to peek inside, despite his usual insistence that he's not a curious person.

"You asked for it that one time, remember?" I smile as I see him register what it is, his face instantly lighting up.

"You said you'd think about it." Dante is genuinely surprised. And aroused—I can tell by the tent forming in his new casual pants.

"I did think about it." I grin mischievously. "Now that your shoulder is virtually healed, I imagine we can have a bit more fun."

"Seriously? I've always wanted to know what it feels like."

"Be careful what you wish for, darling." I grin, rubbing my hand over his erection.

Dante groans softly. "I want this *so* bad," he confesses, whining as he melts beneath my touch like butter under a warm knife.

"I can tell." I gently smack his bulge and Dante bends over with a grunt, holding his privates protectively.

"You make me so happy," he gasps between hurried breaths as he tries to regain his composure.

"So, what are you doing right now? Want to experiment with your new toys?" Patience has never been my virtue.

Dante doesn't need time to think, his answer is immediate. "It's my birthday, isn't it? I can't think of a better gift."

"Oh, so *now* you want gifts?" I laugh. "Fair enough." I kiss him sweetly on the lips—the last drop of sweetness before the strict teacher takes the reins.

I take the box from him and order him to kneel. Like the good boy he is, Dante bends down before me submissively, handing me his body to command.

It's play time!

CHAPTER TWENTY-FOUR

DESIRES

DANTE...

My heart is beating so fast, it feels like it might pop out of my chest any moment now. The anticipation is killing me, but Danica takes her time.

My cock is painfully hard, but there is nothing I can do about it. My limbs are spread to the corners of the bed, restrained by the cuffs that hold them. Naked and exposed, ready for my Queen to do whatever she wants to do to my body. And what she wants is pleasure, *my* pleasure.

Trust Danica to find an island kink hotel that rents fully kitted-out playrooms. The things money can buy...

The *gift*, though, she'd bought herself. I hadn't expected it at all.

The ocean outside is reduced to a gentle salty breeze streaming through the fully drawn blinds, transforming the grand room into a dungeon. Perfectly dimmed mood lighting illuminates the space and lights up my naked body as a humble offering to my Owner.

Danica stands beside the bed, dressed in thick rubber boots and a leather corset-and-panty set she'd brought for this exact moment. *Oh god, she looks stunning. My little devil woman.*

"You know your safe words, right?" she asks, same as always, switching us both into play mode officially. That question always gives my mind permission to let go, to just float into the safe space we've created.

"Yes, Miss. Tap twice on the headboard..."

"Good boy." She flashes me that million-dollar smile, rewarding my needy cock with a firm squeeze. The combination of her praise and her touch sends me wild with desire!

I groan—a loud, primal sound that reverberates through the room—as I try to arch my hips into her grip, desperate to be touched. But she leaves me wanting more, pulling away too soon. *Fanculo!*

"We'll start slow..."

Danica flicks the switch on the wand, and a light buzzing sound fills the room—the soft hum of electricity flowing. It's not a very big device; it looks a bit like an electric toothbrush (maybe thicker on the handle).

An assortment of electrode attachments lay ready on the table beside her, but for now, Danica's hands are all she needs—*she* is the conductor.

A small metal plate is tucked into the front of her corset, holding it in place against her skin; the other side is strapped to her hip in a leather holster and plugged into the wall. She carefully goes through the steps, making sure she sets it up safely.

"What does it feel like?" I ask as Danica holds her hands up to her eyes to see if she can see anything different. But they look the same as always, normal—just hands. There's nothing normal about the electricity flowing through her body though.

"That's *my* question to ask, isn't it?" She smiles, twirling her fingers in the air like a mad scientist about to embark on a grand experiment, and in a way, she is. "You ready, darling?"

"Touch me, please." I want her to ignite me.

I've always been curious about electro-stimulation, especially with so many new and elegant options on the market; so many attachments to play with. But there'd been no one I could trust—until now. I trust Danica fully, not only with my body but with my mind as well.

The violet wand is on its lowest setting; Danica checks it again to make sure. Such a simple device yet such a world of possibility, especially with the body contact cable turning her into the conductor.

It's nerve-wracking but I am calm, ready. I know Danica has read all the instructions, even watched the tutorials. She'd even tried it on herself before, she told me, to gauge its impact—but it wasn't her vibe, not for pleasure at least. Using it to torture me on the other hand? Well, that she can get behind.

I am desperate to know what it feels like. My cock is virtually dripping and Danica hasn't even touched me yet.

She takes a deep breath before slowly moving her hand closer to my upper arm, trailing her fingers over my skin without ever touching it, just a quick flick.

Sparks, literal sparks, crackle as a sharp bite nicks into my skin. It tickles almost. My heart beats faster but it doesn't help regulate my frozen breaths.

Just like in the tutorial, Danica moves her hand down my arm, never touching me, leaving a little gap between my skin and hers for the electricity to spark into my body.

"Can you feel it?" she asks, briefly holding a finger over my nipple. The current cuts into me with a sharp bite.

I gasp. "It feels amazing." It does.

She turns the device off and increases the intensity slightly. When she turns it back on, I know things are about to get serious.

My leg twitches as Danica hovers her fingertip, just a forefinger, over my feet. She touches my big toe, then the top of my foot, my ankle, little taps following a path up my right leg, my knee, my thigh…

Oh god! I hold my breath as she taps her finger on my inner thigh. It stings. Just a sharp, quick jab. *She's so close.* The anticipation is thick in my throat, almost choking me.

And then it happens. I scream as Danica taps a finger on my erect shaft. The sharp jolt of electricity pinches the skin. It burns! But as soon as her finger moves away, I want it there again. The after-burn is addictive. Almost like getting a tattoo but at the same time, nothing like it.

"Do you like that, baby?" Danica coos, studying the expressions on my face. For her, I let it all show. I don't hide anything like I used to.

She reads my body like a book, reaching out to the tip of my hardness with her electric finger. I don't answer, I just groan loudly as the sensitive skin catches alight.

"Look how you twitch and squirm for me, so powerless." An evil cackle escapes her lips but I know I'm safe.

"Does it hurt?"

"More!" I demand, sealing my own fate as Danica reaches for my balls.

FUCK!

The shock would've knocked me off my feet if I wasn't lying down. My whole body convulses as the incredible shock takes the wind right out of my chest.

Danica gives me a moment to catch my breath, enjoying the reactions unfolding before her. So much power in those little hands, that petite frame. If she wants to, she can end me right now and I would be powerless. She can do with me what she wants, consensually or not, but I know she won't. Still, the thought that she *can* is incredibly arousing.

"Don't you dare come without permission, boy." She smacks my cock with four fingers. The greater surface area spreads out the sensation over my skin, hitting my flesh with a sharp jolt. It's not as much of a sting as the single finger, but the smack itself still hurts.

I growl like a primal ape, roaring as I let it all out, everything I've kept inside for so long. All the anger, all the hurt, the pain, all the times I've had to be the strong one, show no fear, I purge it from my body, one shock at a time, as Danica punishes my body for its sins.

Danica touches a nipple in between her forefinger and thumb and my noises grow louder than I've ever allowed myself before. Like a caged beast, I tug at the constraints around my limbs while she pokes and prods little shocks all over my exposed body.

For a second, Danica pulls away, the reprieve only temporary as she increases the wand's intensity setting. She looks at me and I nod. *Do it.*

Without a second thought, Danica goes straight for my cock and my whole body explodes in pain. I'm on fire! It feels like a knife is cutting through my skin. The sting empties my entire mind with its pulse, closing the walls around my reality to just Danica, just the electricity, the pain, the tingle of the dangerous pleasure...

I grunt, unable to find the words to let her know I'm on the edge, so close to coming. The pain is almost unbearable, but not as unbearable as my need to release.

"Not so fast, baby." She knows my body, its signs. "I've got other plans for that cum." She pinches the tip of my cock in a move that sends me into an oblivion of pain. *Oh god.*

Then Danica turns off the device, her fingers instantly just fingers again.

She grins. "Now a little gift for myself..."

CHAPTER TWENTY-FIVE

GIFTS

DANICA...

W atching him intently, I let Dante cool off for a minute. He clearly needs it.

As I unclasp his ankles and wrists, they drop to the bed, limp. His cock is still twitching, so close to orgasm, but left unsatisfied just before its big moment.

How beautiful he looks like this, a beautiful mess—*my* beautiful mess. Lovingly, I stroke Dante's cheek, and he instinctively flinches, expecting electricity. But my skin is no longer electric.

While my darling boy figures out how to breathe in a steady pace again, I fetch a box from my suitcase, a smaller one. It is already open. I'd tried it on earlier, just to see what it was like. It had worked *exactly* how I'd hoped.

I throw the lube down next to Dante before climbing onto the bed, standing over my hungry Knight as he regards me with those awe-filled eyes. He keeps my gaze while I discard what little clothing I have on my body, finally freeing my breasts from their tight confines. They droop over my waist slightly, resting against my body—right where they belong.

Dante still doesn't know what's in the second box. Without breaking eye contact, I take out its contents and drop the box on the bed. Slowly, I sink fingers into my cunt to feel if I'm wet enough—I am.

As I hold Dante's gaze ransom, I slide the short end of the expensive silicone vibrating dildo into myself until the front stands out like a cock of my own. A ribbed bit on top rests perfectly against my clit. Carefully, I slide the custom panties over the dildo, harnessing it against my body to keep it all in my place—just like I'd practiced.

With newfound power, I stand over Dante, letting him admire my new purple cock. It's bigger than the one I usually peg him with but not bigger than his own.

"Do you like it?" I ask, looking down at him.

"You look magnificent." He looks at me in wonder, like I'm the only person in the entire world. It makes me feel brave, powerful.

"And how magnificent will I look pounding your ass into oblivion?"

"Please…" Dante virtually whimpers, his own cock still ready and close to release.

I kneel over him, lowering my new dick to his face. "Why don't you start by wetting this for me, darling?"

Without question, Dante takes me into his mouth as I thrust my hips forward, fucking his face as he gags on my length, almost choking.

"Slowly," I urge, pulling Dante's hair and moving his face.

He nods, sucking on the 7-inch strap-on that is so much more than just a strap-on.

"There you go, such a good boy." I kiss the top of his head, then pull his face off my cock and kiss him deeply, sloppily, as he gasps for breath. "Come here," I order, and Dante shuffles his body down the bed until his ass is on the edge. Making him comfortable, I slip a pillow under him.

Spread in a power stance, I stand between his thighs, resting my cock next to his. I rub them both together, feeling Dante grow to full hardness again.

"Let's warm you up, darling."

Dante gasps as the cold lube hits his hole, even more so when I slip my finger inside his ass to prep him, stretch him. Then two fingers. I wiggle them, finding my way to the nerve endings around his prostate, activating them with the mere flick of my fingers.

I love it when he groans like that, melting into the bed under my touch.

"Are you ready, baby boy? Ready to take my cock?" I rest the tip of the purple member at his hole, letting the anticipation sink in as I draw out my sentence seductively.

"Fuck me, please. I'm ready."

There is something so mesmerizing about seeing such a powerful man so desperate for my touch, something I can never grow tired of.

I push Dante's legs against his chest, lifting his bum into the air so I can guide my strap-on into him, slowly, carefully.

"Relax, darling. Just breathe," I coach him through all the steps he always instantly forgets when we get to this point.

Dante takes a deep breath, unclenching.

"There you go, look how exquisitely you open up for me. Are you going to take it all?" I coo encouragingly, almost patronizingly.

Dante nods, groaning loudly as I push in all the way. For a moment, we just stay like that, unmoving.

He locks his legs around my hips, behind my back, holding me against him as I reach for the remote, turning the dildo into a vibrator, pulsing inside us both—and over my clit. We moan at the same time.

"Now you listen carefully, my darling boy." I lean down, whispering. "Here's what's about to happen. I'm going to fuck you senseless and you're going to blow your load over my breasts like a good boy, is that understood?"

"Oh god," Dante moans, his cock jumping at the mere suggestion. A beautiful flutter of surprise slips from his lips before he composes himself again. "Yes, Ma'am."

"That's what I thought." With a smirk, I slowly pull out until only the tip is left inside his ass. Time for more lube. Holding onto Dante's thighs, I push back in, all the way, vibrating inside him.

The stimulation on my clit is so powerful, as is the vibration inside me. Every time I plunge back into Dante, it pushes against my clit harder, buzzing pleasure into my body.

He doesn't last; he's been on the edge too long. "I can't. Please..." Dante cries, clenching to try and keep the cum from exploding all over himself.

I lean down, pressing my breasts around his cock, rubbing it up and down slowly. "You have permission, my love. Come for me. Let me have every last drop of you."

I wrap my hands around his throat, squeezing with every ounce of strength as I continue thrusting inside him. Dante gasps for breath but I hold on, choking him, riding him until, moments later, he exclaims loudly, swearing in Italian as he releases his spunk all over my chest.

The orgasm between my own thighs quickly builds and I keep fucking him through his cries of overstimulation, riding him until my body contorts in pleasure over him, my skin on fire as the orgasm rips through my veins.

Wave after wave of pleasure crashes down on me. I struggle to find the remote to turn the dildo off as we both become too sensitive to continue.

It finally stops vibrating and I pull out carefully, collapsing into Dante's arms, our bodies heaving up and down together as we try to catch our breath.

Content, I weave my fingers through his, holding his hand as I close my eyes.

"Happy birthday, baby," I tell him but Dante can't speak yet, he just holds me close as my fingers tap against his chest in the rhythm of his heartbeat—my favorite sound.

Chapter Twenty-Six

INSATIABLE

Dante...

"This is torture," I complain to Danica, pulling her naked body closer to mine. Her skin is the only blanket I need; we haven't even gotten dressed yet after her glorious birthday present surprise. Not that I mind the lack of clothing, it sure beats the ridiculous clothing she made me buy.

"This? I've literally shocked your balls with electricity today and you think *this* is torture? We're only on the second episode." Danica laughs, playfully hitting me with a pillow.

"I thought aftercare was supposed to be soothing to me? There is nothing soothing about *Parks & Rec*, I'm sorry." I cross my arms over my chest the way Danica always does when she's upset, pushing a pretend huff through my lips.

"You silly man, you should get us more snacks!" Danica laughs heartily, nestling her head in the pit of my arm. "And more water. Hydration is important."

"What happened to it being *my* birthday? Aren't *I* supposed to be the one who gets service?"

"Didn't you get enough service? Besides, I thought you don't do birthdays."

"Okay, fine. If they're always going to be like this one, maybe I'll reconsider," I tease, pulling Danica closer for a kiss.

Absentmindedly, I run my finger over the jagged scar forming on her arm, the one she got that night of the warehouse ambush. I hate that it's there, that she carries this mark, that someone dared to lay a finger on my Danica. But, at the same time, I love running my fingers over the permanent reminder that she came for me, that she cared enough to risk her life for me.

I press my lips to her broken skin, holding it in a soft kiss.

Hopefully, this saga is all behind us now. Don Ricci personally apologized for his son's disrespectful behavior in kidnapping another Don, vowing to punish him accordingly—and proposed a truce between the families, once more. He says he had no idea, and considering everything my own brother hid from me, I can believe him.

Just in case, I've asked Emilio to upgrade our security at home while we're away.

Having Emilio run things a bit while I recover has been so nice. My brain needed the break as much as my body did. For so long, I've been on autopilot, pushing through the days, the weeks, the years like they were endless, empty.

But I don't want to waste any more of my life, not when I can spend it with Danica. She gives me a reason to get up, to carry on. No matter how much time we spend together, I still can't predict what she'll do next, and it's the most exciting thing. Who thought I'd have so many firsts left to explore at the ripe old age of 43? *You're 44 now*, I remind myself.

"I already know what I'm getting you for your birthday next year." Danica grins mischievously as she tugs at my chest hair like it doesn't hurt. But I like the sensation. "And I'm not telling you, so don't even ask," she adds quickly.

"You're going to make me wait a whole year? You cruel woman."

"I thought I was your Queen?"

"You are. My evil Queen." Too quick for her to get out of the way, I jump on top of her, pinning her body beneath me as I cover her in tickles. Danica squirms around, laughing so hard that she can hardly breathe.

But she quickly gets the upper hand, grabbing my sleeping dick and calling me to order. "I've been called worse."

Throwing my hands up in the air, I surrender, rolling onto my back. But she doesn't let go, oh no.

"I wouldn't want you any other way. You're perfect." I kiss her nose.

For a moment, we just lie like that, her hand lazily playing with my half-sleeping cock like she's petting a dog. There is nowhere I have to be, nowhere I'd rather be, than right here.

Everything around me feels light, breezy almost—not just the temperature but the tension in my shoulders, the pressure at the back of my throat…This unexpected state of contentment is warm in my belly.

How effortlessly Danica waltzed into my life, merging our completely different worlds like they were always meant to intertwine, two puzzle pieces finally interlocking. I didn't have to change myself to fit her, to overthink my next move to be agreeable to her—I could just be, and I was exactly who I needed to be.

"I love you," I whisper into her hair, breathing in her scent.

My unexpected confession catches us both by surprise. But I don't regret it.

Danica pushes herself up onto her elbows to look at me intently. She is pensive for a moment, searching my eyes for the sincerity I know she finds.

I smile almost sheepishly, feeling even more vulnerable in this moment than I did spread out naked and tied up on the bed before her.

She touches my cheek affectionately as she smiles, telling me with her eyes as much as her words: "My darling *Tesoro*, I love you too."

Overwhelmed by emotion, I kiss her deeply, taking her face in both hands as I bite her bottom lip gently.

"So many birthday presents. How lucky am I?"

"Care for one more?" My not-so-soft-anymore cock jumps to attention as Danica flicks her fingers over the tip, trailing her long red nails over the skin carefully.

"You're insatiable, woman!" It's a statement of fact more than an accusation.

"Is that a yes?"

"Oh god, yes. Please, Miss."

Danica drags a sharp nail over my shaft, over my balls, and I hold my breath. She smiles mischievously, reaching for the lube on the bedside. "I thought as much, baby boy..."

A loud grunt bellows from my insides as she pinches my cock between her fingers in a move that is both painful and incredibly arousing. *How does she do that?*

"Hmm, I have this thing I want to try. Hold on, let me get my phone. I saved a screenshot somewhere." Danica jumps off the bed without waiting for a response, determined as always.

"As long as it isn't more *Parks & Rec*," I call after her, drawing an annoyed grunt from Danica in the other room.

Smiling, I put my hands behind my head like a pillow and lie back, waiting for my Queen to return with whatever treat or torture she has in mind.

Perhaps I can learn to like birthdays after all.

Want more Danica & Dante content? Read Book 3 (*Valentine for Dante*), or unlock the free *Domme vs Don* short by joining my monthly newsletter via mkaynoir.com/newsletter

THANK YOU

Thank you for reading my book.

If you enjoyed it, wouldn't you please take a moment to leave me a **review** at your favorite retailer? It helps more like-minded people to find this very niche content.

Do you want more stories with this vibe? Then carry on reading...

To get bonus content and fresh releases, join my **newsletter**(via mkaynoir.com/newsletter) or follow me on **BookBub**.

Kay

MORE BY M KAY NOIR

Valentine for Dante

Queens & Knights Book 3

***

Torn between desire and duty, I'm frozen.

Danica and I are so happy together.

So, why now? Why are you here?

This won't end well...

I can't want this.

I shouldn't.

But I do.

***

More info and links via mkaynoir.com/dante

ABOUT THE AUTHOR

M Kay Noir is a queer romance author and journalist obsessed with moments of desire. Most of her stories are kinky, queer-friendly, polyamorous undertakings with neurotic characters who are often their own worst enemy. If you expect any regard for traditional gender roles or power dynamics, you will be disappointed.

Kay has been penning steamy moments for more than 15 years now, from fanfics to ghostwriting and now finally her own stories. Her day job also involves a lot of writing, albeit a different kind—mostly sustainability things. When she's not writing (or reading), she enjoys making her husband look at yet another sunset and watching live music concerts.

**See mkaynoir.com for the long version.